PATIENT 2.5.7

Chapter One: 1935 – A Special Little Girl

The building was tall and leered at the grounds it was surrounded by. Made of stone, it stood silently like it was waiting for something but everyone knew what lived inside. Madness was a scary, uncontrollable urge that needed an understanding and especially in the era of the 1930s, onlookers feared what lied within. It was a time when this sort of building was left to its own devises. Only the people who worked there came and went. It was bordered by a large stone wall with high metal gates that gave the whole setting its prestige and respect.

The hallways and corridors were walled with white paint and green tiled flooring shined a reflection of the patients and staff that walked through. There were four floors altogether, with each having rooms with medical supplies and then bedrooms. These bedrooms were numbered. They were numbered from one hundred to three hundred.

As a little girl sat on a bench facing a window within the hospital on the ground floor, she swung her legs back and fore unable to reach the floor when fully seated. Her dress was a basic brown but had dark stains all over it, and her socks were a grubby white like she had been running shoeless in mud. Her hair was platted to the side, but her split ends were shown by the frays of the untidiness of the plat. The colour of her hair was even more abnormal. It was an almost white. Her eyes were the palest colour. Her right was a pale blue and her left was a pale green. It was only noticeable when studied closely and as the light shone onto her face from the window, her eyes twinkled.

She picked up an old notebook and pencil that was resting next to her along the bench and she watched out the window. Her innocence was heightened her nervousness. She was only six and when she heard an old man clear his throat, she jumped with a shiver running down her spine like someone had walked on her grave. She turned her head with a tilt and an innocently wild expression appeared on her face. Her eyes and nose were still red from her tears. The old man had sat next to her with the creaking of his old bones. She smiled at him like she knew him; the sound of the bones creaking was comforting to her.

"Now my child, do you know where you are?" asked the old man. He had very grey hair, wearing an old blue suit. It looked a little scruffy, like it was very old, yet it wasn't the normal style a man would wear during the 1930s. The scent of old moth balls aired through the little girl's nostrils as she answered him.

"No Sir, but am I to stay?"

"Yes," he breathed. "This is where you belong now." He turned to look at the people behind them. The little girl also redirected her gaze and saw her mother and her father talking to a man in a white coat. The strange man looked stern and sent a nervy chill down the little girl's spine. A lady with a uniform joined them. Her hat was quite frilly. The little girl turned back to the old man as he spoke again. "I need you to remember something for me."

"Yes Sir?"

"I cannot stay here with you, but I need you to be wary of the people you may meet. You are a very special little girl and these people won't understand you. But there is someone coming for you. Can you remember that for me?"

"I can try," she muttered, glancing at the people behind her. "Are you going back with them?" she gestured to her parents.

The old man had a solemn expression. "No. But you already know that, do you not?" He gave her a little wink.

"Will you stay with me for a little while longer then?" the girl ignored his observation.

"That is not possible I am afraid," Grandpa thought for a moment. "I will always be with you in spirit." This time he spoke with a distance, like he had moved away, although he hadn't. The little girl lowered her head and looked at the blank page and the old man finally advised, "Always understand the difference between truth and exaggeration. Draw pictures and it will help you and it help the person coming for you."

The next time the little girl turned to look up at his wrinkled old face, the old man was gone; like a memory; like a ghost. She leaned onto her knees and faced the group of people that were still talking. Her father left first without a glance in her direction and her mother took one last look at her daughter. The little girl felt the loneliness set in as she smiled with hope and raised her hand with a gentle wave. Her mother did not wave back. In fact her expression was a definitive disapproving stare that would lock into the little six-year-old's memory like an obsession.

Once they were out of sight, the man in the white coat strode to her side. He was tall; very tall. And thin; almost sickly thin. He did not speak but motioned for the little girl to follow. As she did so, her socks oozed a muddy red puddle around her feet. As she walked it produced similar footprints. The little girl gulped at the sight and he reassured her that everything was going to be alright now that she was there. They reached a door after walking up many flights of stairs and around many corridors. The woman with the uniform was stood next to it. It might have been a different woman with the same uniform, the little girl was unsure.

“This is your room now,” said the lady and she stepped inside with her. She looked at her up and down, noticing just how dirty the little girl was. On her hands, the mud had dried. “Take off your clothes for burning and I’ll come and fetch you for your scrub down.” The lady locked the girl inside her room, 2.5.7.

Chapter Two: 2014 – An Old Doctor's Story

"Excuse me nurse, could you tell me where Richard Pearce's room is? It's my first day and I'm supposed to keep him company?" asked a young woman at the reception desk of the nursing home for the elderly. She had parked her car just outside in one of the many parking spaces and once she had locked the car door, she realised she had forgotten her bag and had to return to get it. She took a few puffs of her e-cigarette and walked inside. The nurse had seen her from her position by the reception desk.

"You're one of the new carers?" The nurse smiled back in a 'customer service' sort of way and checked on the computer.

"My name is Kirsty, Kirsty Biggs."

"Yes I was told. I'll take you to him." The nurse looked back down at the screen for a moment and endlessly tapped the keyboard seemingly searching for something that must not be there, until finally the nurse stood and walked around the desk to Kirsty's side. "Come, I will show you."

They reached his room in no time as the place was quite small and the nurse knocked lightly. An old man's voice grunted enter. "Ah Richard," the nurse said condescendingly. "You have a visitor today." Kirsty noticed him role his eyes as the nurse spoke. He was sitting at his table in front of an old typewriter. He was wearing an old man suit without the tie. "He's been wearing his old suits for a while now."

Once the nurse left them alone. Kirsty took off her coat and sat on the end of the bed. "So how are you Richard?"

"I'm fine." He remained slumped at his desk.

"My name's Kirsty," she plonked her bag onto the bed and her e-cigarette fell out.

"Hmm," he did not look up from his typewriter. He just stared at it contemplating. "Smoking is bad for you."

"Feeling a little down today?" She tried to change the subject.

"No."

"Then what is wrong?" She folded her arms.

"The nurses think I need company so they hire you people to sit with me and talk to me like I'm a child." Kirsty noticed his hands trembling. "So go on offer a boring game of chess or cards."

"Well, I won't speak to you like a child. You are older than me after all. And I don't like chess." Richard didn't answer. She saw him struggling to type. "Why don't you get a laptop? It would be a lot easier." She moved closer to him and her voice had softened. "You can borrow mine?"

“NO.” he snapped. With an awkward pause his voice cleared and became mollified as hers had done. “Sorry. It’s just the typewriter was hers. And I don’t understand those stupid computers.”

“Who’s typewriter was it?”

“The typewriter belongs to my wife.”

Kirsty took his arm to help him stand and sat him in the armchair by the window. “Do you have a picture? What was she like?”

“Pretty, lovely, caring.” He went silent. It hurt him to talk about her, although he had lost her now three years ago. He took out his wallet from his inner pocket and pulled out an old crumpled photograph.

“She’s pretty,” Kirsty studied the photo. It was from the early 1960s. “What were you typing anyway?”

“My career,” Richard paused. “She told me I needed to tell me story before I can see her again.”

“I’ll type for you if you want me to or I’m a good listener?” She sat in his place at the table and looked at the papers he had been typing. A lot of the words were smudged by Richard’s clumsiness with the wet ink. “Memoirs of being a doctor?”

“I realised while writing my memoirs, that there wasn’t much point if I couldn’t tell the whole truth.”

"You mean because you'd be breaking doctor-patient confidentiality?" Kirsty was confused.

"No. I mean I would be lying if I said that all my work was down to me. My career was a journey that started with my first patient and even ended with that same patient all those years later. I am writing the truth. I am writing her story. She deserves that."

"Her story? I'm a little confused?"

"My first patient's story."

"First patient?"

"Yes. Only I and she knew what really happened and I think that's what my wife wanted me to write. It's so I don't forget. I must never forget about her."

"What sort of doctor were you?" Richard gave her a stern glance. "I mean are?"

"I started with psychology and ended in Forensics."

Kirsty had always been interested in medicine but never managed to get the qualifications. Richard was a psychiatrist with an understanding of surgery. He had worked in many hospitals in his career, which started when he was just twenty five. He was eighty nine just last Tuesday. Kirsty was hooked by the start. She loved a good story.

"Was your first patient crazy then?" she asked.

Richard laughed. It tickled him. “In some ways but everyone is a little crazy.”

Suddenly, the room door opened. A man entered. He was tall and had dark hair. He was a similar age to Kirsty, about twenty eight and wearing jeans and a t-shirt. “I’m sorry?” he said. “I didn’t realise you have company already?” He stood in the doorway.

“Oh come in, we don’t mind,” Kirsty said kindly. “Are you another new carer?”

“Um, yes.” He stuttered

“I’m Kirsty and this is Richard.”

“I’m Joe.”

“So you’re both staying?” Richard rolled his eyes.

“Well I’m sure Joe wants to hear your story too.” Kirsty looked at Joe who perched himself on the bed and he acknowledged.

Richard groaned and that old man in the arm chair by the window, who used to be Doctor Richard Pearce, psychiatrist, cleared his throat. “You know this story is where I first met my wife.”

“Really?” Kirsty had been deep in thought. “Oh by the way,” she said to Joe. “This is about Doctor Pearce and his first patient.”

"Yes," Richard continued. "So if it wasn't for my university professor pushing me into the field of psychology, I may never have met her." He chuckled at the prospect.

"What do you mean push you? Surely you were training as a psychologist in university?"

Richard leaned back in his chair quite comfortably. "To be honest in my school days I could never decide what field I wanted to study. I took a few courses related to the more physical side of medicine, I suppose the surgical side. Then for extra credit I took a class in psychology, where my professor felt I could develop my skills further."

"Should I be typing this?" Kirsty interrupted apologetically.

"No this is not really the important bit. Sorry. I know I rattle on."

"I don't mind. I enjoy listening to you."

"Me too," Joe commented.

"You know Kristy reminds me of my wife when she says that."

"Why's that?" Joe asked.

"She often said that to me when I would explain things. She often assisted me in some of my consultations later on in years actually."

"Shall we continue then?" Kirsty was thinking about time. This was only supposed to be a day visit, and it felt like it was going to be a long story.

"The story starts at my first job in the asylum. I've held these secrets within my mind about the place for so long, that it feels like I am doing something wrong now. If it wasn't for the first patient I had within the wretched place, I would not have been the doctor I became. Obviously, this first case study involved psychology, after getting the placement with the help of my university professor. He helped me and another newly qualified doctor get jobs there."

"So you know when you say asylum, is it like the ones in the horror movies because when was this? 19-"

"1955 was when I started, and this place was a lot worse that those ones you see in the movies."

"So this patient of yours was misunderstood? Why was she in a mental asylum when she wasn't mad?" Kirsty asked

"Oh she was mad, just not insane. But that is a long story."

"Start at the beginning then."

"After being instructed that I had been given the opportunity to work in the asylum as my professor was close friends with the head doctor, Doctor De Ville, I made my way from my tiny apartment that was right next to my university, to the outskirts of the town of Oxford where the asylum was positioned. I suppose the journey from my apartment to the asylum took about an hour by bus. On my first day, I jumped off the bus and it was a short walk from my stop. It was quiet along the streets, I remember, due to the earliness of my trip. There weren't that many cars in those days anyway, but it was very quiet that early. You can imagine what I was wearing as well in the fifties: a typical smart suit and tie with a matching hat and case. And back then I was young with tidy dark hair and a clean shaven face; not like now with all this grey.

I had my case in one hand and my hat in the other; it was quite warm I recall. Finally, I reached the high metal gates of the asylum. I tried to push the gate but was shut tight. I noticed it needed a lick of paint as some of it crumbled in my hand. Suddenly a guard came out of a little hut and walked up to the gate from inside the grounds. His hut was attached to a separate building from the main one. It looked newer.

"You one of them new doctors?" he asked. He was an older gentleman, with scruffy whiskers around his mouth. I just nodded and he unlocked the gate, allowing me to step inside. I wasn't sure whether I was meant to wait for him so I slowly started to edge to the building. "The other doc has already arrived," the guard spoke with a musing air and I paused to wait for him. He continued, "He seemed a bit up himself in my opinion."

I chuckled. "Sounds like him," I mentioned. Doctor Mackenzie was a peer of mine at the time and he had also been given the chance to join the staff. He was very competitive and I, if I am honest, hated him. He irritated the hell out of me.

"Well, you wanna go to reception and report to Matron. She's a bossy mare mind!" the guard pointed in the direction of reception and began walking back to his hut mumbling to himself. I remember pulling at my collar before taking my next step towards the great stoned building, out of nervousness. "Oh and watch yourself doc, strange things happen in there. That's why I stay out 'ere." He called back to me with a wave of his arms in frustration. "Sometimes if you go in you don't get the option to come back out!"

"Thank you," I mumbled. He was a peculiar man but in some way he put me at ease. I made my way to the entrance. I remember the building was made of a fine stone which was elegant and slightly eerie, but that was more to do with the fact that I knew what was waiting for me inside.

The door was large and made of a thick oak. On it was a brass sign, naming the building as Gravehill Asylum. I gave the door a shove and took my first steps into the asylum that was going to make me the doctor I became. The reception was a clean-ish white colour with a number of chairs along the walls. I strode to the desk that was to my left and had a nurse sitting quietly behind it. After introducing myself she picked up the phone and said something like "they're here." Then she gestured to me to take a seat, which I did although awkwardly. Doctor Mackenzie was also present. He was wearing a better suit than me at the time. To be honest, looking back, I was very jealous of him.

Moments later, I recall the matron entering in a blue and white uniform. She had a stern expression on her wrinkled face, telling us the rules and showing us around the hospital. Doctor Mackenzie walked slightly ahead of me, more in time with Matron but I kept my pace. Walking through the ground floor, there were a number of large communal rooms and one or two public wash rooms. Matron had explained that most of the patients did not use those rooms as they were washed by one of the nurses. We weren't shown every room. I remember Matron saying it wasn't our place to know.

We walked up a flight of stairs; the first lot of bedrooms; some on the right hand side of the corridor and some on the left were all uniformed. As we walked, I noticed the doors were thick and strong looking with numbers on them that, from my point of view, went from one hundred upwards. And when I questioned this to Matron she fobbed me off with some reason I cannot remember now; the real reason being that she did not know.

"Right, so now for the rules for patients and their bedrooms," Matron stated with a clap of her hands and swivelling on the spot to face both me and Doctor Mackenzie. At this point I realised, we must be on about the third floor by now and we were by the room number 3.2.1. My feet were aching. "Patients are in bed by seven, unless they have been logged out by one of the doctors, which means that they can be out as long as nine in the evening. We try to treat their rooms as their own personal spaces, however, sometimes spot checks are necessary and sometimes if we feel they are a danger then that rule is ignored."

I personally took that to mean that the rule for personal space was merely a front to the visitors, rather than a human right. Matron had moved on by the time I began to listen to her again. "Nurses also work on night shifts and are to hand if there came a time you need them. However, they are under my charge not the doctors so I can overrule at any point. This of course is for future reference once you two actually begin working independently from the consultants. Now, as long as you have no questions for me, I will let you explore alone as I need to get on. Meet back at reception for 11 o'clock sharp to meet some of the faculty." Before we could respond, she was walking down the corridor with her back to us.

Doctor Mackenzie smiled at me and we continued to stroll through, peaking through the small cloudy windows of some of the rooms. We discussed psychology as a profession and by my understanding; Doctor Mackenzie seemed very serious about it. I still wasn't sure whether this role was for me. Eventually we got to the top floor, which were the consultant rooms. The first time I had set foot on this floor, I felt an ache in the pit of my stomach. We didn't dare have a peak in them just in case, so returned down the stairs.

"Hey, can you wait a minute for me?" Doctor Mackenzie asked, tossing his thumb behind him at a toilet door.

"I suppose I'll have to," I replied, leaning against the wall to wait for him.

"I won't be long!" he jogged in. I stood in the corridor alone, when all of a sudden, in the corner of my eye, I saw something move. When I turned my head the corridor was empty, but still now I could have sworn I had seen something. I walked carefully onwards to double check my own sanity. To explain, the corridors weren't actually straight, they bended slightly so one could not see straight ahead of them; creepy is probably the best the word to describe it. I stopped by one of the rooms and for some reason I decided to look through the cloudy window of number 1.5.4.

BANG!

I rebounded back against the other wall as the patient in 1.5.4 screamed and wailed at the sight of me. I had knocked into a door behind me and the patient within that room also began to scream. As I stood in the centre of the corridor I remember stressing about my next move. And as I lingered, more patients began to scream around me!

I tried to walk back to the toilets that Doctor Mackenzie had gone into but with all the noise I lost my bearings, crumbling to the floor and holding my hands over my ears. I did not know which way to go.

"You're lost." a woman's voice spoke softly. My heart was beating out of my chest at this point and I was glad just to see sight of another person. I stood up from crouching and saw a woman standing in the corridor. She was wearing a gown and her hair was most peculiar colour of white I had ever seen. It was not grey; it was like a blonde white that you could no longer class as blonde. I noticed she had a band around her arm but was unable to read it by the angle she was on.

"I-I," I found myself stuttering and she tilted her head like she was calculating me or observing me. I will always remember that look she gave me. It was so meaningful, even caring you could describe it, but full of an untouchable deepness that put me uneasy. As if she was looking into my own soul and understanding me better than I could ever comprehend.

She lifted her finger to her lip and hushed me. I found the patients within the rooms had also calmed. It was funny really because as soon as I caught sight of this woman the screaming had ceased from my ears like a deafening blast. Her eyes were glassy and her face so pale from the lack of sunlight. I wanted to touch her, just to see if she was real.

I tried to step towards her but suddenly I felt a hand placed on my shoulder! As I jumped and turned back it was only Doctor Mackenzie, who laughed at my reaction. "Looks like you've seen a ghost or something?" he chuckled.

I looked back to where the woman had been, but she was gone; just a memory of once was; a blur. "I think I did," I had mumbled quietly enough for him to not hear me and we continued to reception in order not to get into any more trouble."

"Was that your first patient? The one in the corridor then?" Kirsty interrupted. She had been lost within the story from when it began. She was enthralled.

Richard looked up almost startled, like he had forgotten Kirsty and Joe were there. He nodded his old head and continued. "Although I tried to forget about the strange encounter, it stayed with me throughout my introduction to the hospital; and yes I was to meet that woman again. From this point of my first day, we were abruptly introduced to some of the nurses that were on shift at that time and then the consultants. It later became time to meet some of the patients in which I was to meet my intriguing first case study officially. As you probably have guessed, as soon as I stepped inside this asylum I knew my loyalties would change dramatically. However, from this moment on from seeing the ghostly figure in the corridor, it's like the story has a life of its own, like you are transported back to the fifties just by imaging her. Sanity and insanity become twisted and partnerships and relationships become confusing.

Imagine a younger handsome version of myself, who can actually stand tall. Dark hair compared to this grey thin rug on my head now. Having a professional briefcase, hat and coat. A man eager to make a difference in the world of medicine, until he comes to this asylum and meets his first patient. That's when things change.

Imagine the looming building that stood eerily in the middle of its grounds it had, containing the studies of the mind; the insane, the crazy and the simply misunderstood. And imagine the patient I was about to meet – Patient 2.5.7 – because this story opens your mind to its full potential. On continuing this true story, you can never go back. You will know the truth even if you may never understand it.

PART ONE:

THE ASYLUM

Chapter Three: August 1955 – Meeting the Staff of Gravehill

Richard and Mackenzie had reached the reception and waited an hour for Matron to return to them. They did not converse in much conversation together as Mackenzie had picked up a newspaper that was on a stack of them on the side table of the seats. The nurse that was sat behind reception was filling out some sort of paperwork and ignored the both of them. Richard, for a while had been staring at the sickening green coloured tiles on the floor, until a noise perked up his attention further inside the hospital. From reception or rather the visitors waiting area, was a door with glass walls either side leading into one of the communal rooms. It was probably the communal rooms for visitors. There had been no patients in sight since he arrived that morning. Only the ones that had startled him within their bedrooms.

Two nurses had appeared in the communal room with a patient. The patient was a man with a number strapped onto his arm by a cloth band, reading 1.1.2 on it. He was wearing thin clothed trousers and shirt, like pyjamas. He was barefooted and crying and blubbering uncontrollably, which Richard felt unsettling but the nurses did not seem to mind. Suddenly the crying patient screamed as if in agony, "she touched me! She touched me!" and the nurses lost their holds of him. He caught the eye of Richard from the other side of the glass walls, who had stood up after the screaming to offer assistance. The patient ran towards him and smacked against the glass wall harshly. The bang echoed through the asylum and the nurses rushed to the patient who was now on the floor. Richard followed, passing through the doorway and tried to assist as the patient was very strong.

One of the nurses advised him to hold him down, while the other nurse inserted a needle into the patient's lower back. The patient's screams ceased. His body went limp and Richard stood up helping the nurse, who was also on the floor. She was about the same age as him, nearing thirty. Her hair was a silky brown along with her eyes and her perfect pear-shaped figure aroused Richard's smile from a weak acknowledgement to a beaming grin.

"Well done Doctor Pearce," said Matron, who had appeared from the corner with a stretcher. "You can help put Patient 1.1.2 on here and Doctor Mackenzie," she called and leaned into the reception doorway, "you can help too." Both doctors lifted the patient onto the stretcher.

Matron, with two porters, walked away with the patient muttering in his doze, "it was her; she touched me."

Richard wondered who he might have been talking about but was even more curious over the fact Matron had called the patient by a number.

He turned to the nurse, who he had helped stand after dealing with the patient. “Excuse me nurse,” he tapped her on the shoulder.

“Nurse Caddy,” she smiled.

Richard’s heart beat a little quicker as she spoke. “Why have the patients got a band round their arms? And numbers?”

She opened her mouth to answer but Matron had returned with what seemed a practiced answer on the tip of her tongue. “Well Doctor Pearce, that is observant of you,” she began. “It is their identification. Every patient has a room number and that is the location to take them to if we ever need to put them in their own safe environment. It is easier than remembering names.”

“I see,” he replied, but wasn’t particularly satisfied with the answer. He felt it best not to pry.

“Now gentlemen,” Matron clapped her hands sharply. “You know who I am and Nurse Gretel, you have already been getting acquainted with.” She gestured to the nurse behind the reception desk. As Matron continued, both Richard and Mackenzie were introduced to a number of nurses, but Richard enjoyed being introduced to Nurse Caddy again.

Richard took her hand like he had done with the other nurses he had been introduced to but a spark shook through his body after taking hers. She had felt it too.

They were interrupted by Mackenzie, who stole her hand away to be introduced as well. After the greetings, Nurse Caddy and another nurse called Nurse Jones took the doctors to be introduced to the other doctors on the top floor.

Mackenzie walked ahead with Nurse Jones making sure he could be introduced first and Richard followed. "My name is Chloe by the way," Nurse Caddy said as she slowed her pace to walk beside him.

"Richard," he replied awkwardly which seemed to amuse her. "I was wondering about that patient?"

"Patient 1.1.2? He's alright normally. Just gets flustered easily."

"But who was he talking about? A nurse?"

"Oh no," she paused for a moment choosing her words carefully it seemed. "Another patient that's all. This patient doesn't get on with the other patients. And they weren't meant to be out of their rooms at the same time."

Finally they reached the offices. In one office, three doctors were gathered. There was Doctor Cunningham; a slightly overweight man with a smart beard and balding scalp. There was another called Doctor Irons; a man who was clean shaven and a lot younger than the other two, but still a little bit older than Richard and Mackenzie. And finally there was Doctor Wainwright, a physically fit man, who's suit looked slightly too tight for his arm muscles. He also had the strongest hand shake, Richard noticed. The office itself was smart, with a lot of knickknacks and a few books. This was Doctor Cunningham's office, the older doctor of the three.

They all welcomed Richard and Mackenzie to the asylum and joked about going insane themselves. "You'll find sometimes that if you haven't slept enough you start seeing the same things as the patients ha!" Doctor Wainwright chuckled.

"But just don't tell us and we won't lock you up!" said Doctor Irons. Although he was joking, both Richard and Mackenzie couldn't help exchanging looks of anxiety as they laughed along. His comment had a threatening tone.

"You must get a lot of nutters then?" Mackenzie commented tactlessly.

The laughter seemed to dwindle slightly and Doctor Cunningham went to his drawer pulling out a bottle of whiskey. "Professionally speaking this job is not for the light hearted lads," he spoke with a concentration as he poured a glass for each doctor.

"Well we didn't really expect that, did we Mackenzie?" Richard answered trying to continue the conversation. "But speaking professionally, what is our role here?"

The three doctors looked to him with the same inquisitive glare until Doctor Cunningham asked, "What do you mean Pearce?"

"Well it is just I, or rather we, have not been told anything about the job and there are only four offices on this floor."

"That is a very good question!" said a firm voice from behind them. Richard almost jumped from the voice and swivelled around with Mackenzie doing the same. It was a doctor in a white coat, unlike the others who were not wearing theirs. They were in their work suits, professional looking, but on seeing the man at the door, they were put to shame. His hair was grey and swept to one side covering a balding scalp. He was very thin and his suit pristinely straight, even his chain of his pocket watch was faultless.

"You must be Doctor Richard Pearce. I recognise you from your professor's description."

"I'm afraid you have me at a disadvantage," Richard replied offering his hand. After a brisk shake, the doctor withdrew his hand and gave it a wipe with his handkerchief.

"This is the senior doctor, Doctor De Ville. We all report to him for guidance." Doctor Cunningham introduced. "He's been part of this place since it was built in 1912."

"You are my professor's friend who was gracious enough to give me this experience," Richard smiled politely.

"That is quite accurate Pearce. Now the other face I do not recognise must be Doctor James Mackenzie. Like déjà vu, Doctor De Ville reacted the same way with Mackenzie's handshake as Richard's.

"De Vil? Is that French?" Mackenzie asked. He became known quite quickly with a tongue quicker than his thoughts.

"It is pronounced *De V ale.*" Doctor De Ville's eyes narrowed as if sizing him up and after a pause, he stated that they were to have a meeting with him individually in his own office, so he can address their roles within the asylum.

Mackenzie was first, so Richard waited outside in the corridor for his turn. It was quite a while to wait, which led him to think about the last time he was in a corridor alone. There were no patients on this floor, but he couldn't help but feel uneasy thinking about seeing the disappearing woman in the corridor again.

He thought about her appearance. The strange colour of her hair and the stare she had given him. So deep. So poignant. He had never been made to feel that way before. It was as if everything had become another world in which he had stepped into a bubble so there was nothing but him and the woman. It was ludicrous of course.

Suddenly, Mackenzie came out of the room, creating an echo by his footsteps stomping away down the corridor towards the stairs.

Then came the strong voice, “Pearce, come in.”

Richard scuttled in and shut the door behind him. De Ville’s office seemed almost regal looking, with a wall of book shelves on one side and a large desk in the centre on the room, with a number of different type chairs to choose from. Richard felt worried about picking the wrong one just in case it showed something psychologically.

There was a large chair behind the desk and had its back to him. He cleared his throat nervously and De Ville could sense his fear. “You’re nervous.” He swivelled round on his chair. “That is expected I suppose, but does not fit your professor’s description of you.”

“Really?” Richard felt he needed to say something even though it was only two syllables.

“Take a seat.”

Richard looked around at the number of chairs; there was a typical couch that was the poshest item in the room, then there were two arm chairs and finally two normal wooden chairs set a distance away from the desk. They seemed like the safest option.

The chair creaked as he sat and it felt like an age before De Ville spoke again. “Well done Doctor Pearce,” he smiled with his fingertips tapping against his other hand’s fingertips. “Mackenzie felt the need to move the chair closer to my desk. Controlling issues you could say. Thoughts?”

“I quite agree doctor,” Richard felt sweat across his brow and resisted the urge to wipe it. “Any diagnosis of me yet Doctor?”

“Hmmm,” he leaned his arms onto his desk. “That needs a further study.”

Richard could only nod in response. The topic turned to the topic at hand; Richard’s place in the hospital. Doctor De Ville explained that Richard was to start with one or two case studies before he became a permanent doctor at the hospital. These case studies were to be patients of his choice, which will be fully reported and presented to De Ville and the other doctors. These patients were to continue with their own doctors and have extra consultations with Richard.

"In these reports, do they include observations as well as official diagnosis?" Richard scratched his chin with thought.

"What do you think?"

"Well judging by your observations of staff it seems logical."

"Your report is your independent study. If you do not wish to reveal all your notes that is your privilege. However, if it is a detail which could cause a definitive change in one's analysis or even another's surely should be told."

"Quite right Sir."

"You also have access to previous notes from either myself or the other doctors dependent of which patient you choose. I do not have many patients anymore, so it is unlikely you will have mine."

De Ville stood up from behind his desk and walked around it. He was in better light. He offered his hand to Richard, who shook it carefully. Richard thanked him for the consultation and saw the deep bags under the doctor's eyes, which were caused by the years of working in the asylum. As he turned and left the room, De Ville said one last thing. "Be careful whom you choose mind," he spoke with an eerie air. Richard turned back to the senior doctor. "We, meaning myself, Cunningham, Irons and Wainwright have particular patients we do our rounds on. If you have one of mine, which as I said unlikely, but if you do, and disagree with me, well," he snickered. "Prepare for a debate."

"I wouldn't expect anything less Sir."

"You will sit in with the doctors first before you choose." He shut the door behind him and took a deep sigh of relief. He was going to have to choose carefully but as he came to realise, patients often choose their own doctors and even more importantly in some cases neither choose; it was something that had to be.

Chapter Four: November 1955 – Choosing The Patient

After months of sitting in with doctors, it was finally time for Richard and Mackenzie to have their own case study. Richard had learnt a lot from the other doctors. He particularly liked sitting in with Doctor Irons as he was the younger of them all, bringing fresh ideas to their role of the patients. Doctor De Ville had not been involved with their training however. Richard had asked Matron when he might sit in with De Ville but she always gave some excuse.

Richard was nervous to think that he soon will have a patient of his own. It didn't help that he was in tight spaces with Mackenzie as both he and Mackenzie were given an office next to Matron's room on the ground floor that was situated near reception. They were forced to share, which Richard already knew was going to be challenging. In the morning, Richard found a note addressed to him by De Ville, to choose his patient by that day while most of the patients had turns in the communal rooms. There was a similar note on the desk with Doctor Mackenzie's name on it too. The day was Tuesday, which usually meant rest days for the patients, so it was quite an upheaval for many of them. The sessions began from one o'clock in the afternoon until half past five.

The time flew by to one o'clock and he reported to reception as the letter had stated and met Nurse Caddy. She smiled at him but with Mackenzie on his heels, Richard could not find courage to talk to her. The clock ticked its last few seconds before one o'clock and like the clockwork, there were sounds of movements from the upstairs.

Nurse Caddy came and stood by Richard. "This is only some of the first floor of patients," she whispered to him. "They will swap over around quarter past two."

"Thank you," he replied. "Only some?"

"Yes, they are not forced to come out, but-"

Suddenly through the glass walls patients moved in unison into the communal rooms. At first there was a large number of them, men and women, but soon they spread through the number of communal rooms that ran throughout the ground floor. "So none of the patients have aggressive tendencies?"

"Not the ones that have come out. I think if you wanted to pick one of those, I assume you would have to request it to Doctor De Ville."

"I think I'll be alright with these." Richard breathed nervously.

"Good luck," Nurse Caddy said brushing passed him as she went on duty to help the nurses who had brought the patients down the stairs.

Moments after the crowd had dispersed, Doctor De Ville appeared. He gestured for them to come through and both Richard and Mackenzie followed him through the number of communal rooms. Richard smelt the stench of stuffy air within the rooms.

"Doctors," he began. "You address each patient by their number and you give me their number as soon as you have decided. I will then address you on rules regarding those specific patients as some have routine." He paused for a moment and took a deep breath. "Oh and try not to ask too many questions. It puts a lot of them uneasy and as they are not used to being out with all these characters, then it is best to keep things simple."

As Richard walked behind both De Ville and Mackenzie he noticed that all the patients were of the one hundreds and no more. "I take it the *one* that is part of their number is the floor they are on?"

De Ville stopped immediately with Mackenzie almost walking into him. He twirled with a squeak of his shoe and gave the young doctor a stern look before replying, "Well done again Pearce. You seem to observe well." He left them in the middle of one of the communal rooms and Richard heard Mackenzie say something under his breath.

“Kissass.” was the remark.

Richard rolled his eyes and continued through the rooms. Most of them were bare and contained little entertainment. There was a television in one room, which seemed to be popular. Many patients stared mindlessly.

There were a number of seats within this room and some play things in the corner. There was a layer of dust on them too. Mackenzie had moved quickly; he looked at each patient for a few moments and moved on. Richard, however, watched from afar. He did not know where to begin. There were about 20 in this room alone.

He stepped slowly but with a certain doctor sway having his hands behind his back and his feet lifting in rhythm with his sway. He came across a man who was hunched and deformed. He found his appearance interesting. He couldn’t seem to form sentences. He moved on after the patient had lost interest in him. He noticed a woman sitting on the ground with her legs crossed. He smiled at her, but she barked like a dog. Richard couldn’t help but jump back with surprise and decided it was best to leave her to it. When he turned back to the man, deformed, he decided against him. He moved on.

The time ran away and soon the patients from the first floor were returned to their rooms. The second lot looked the same as the others. There were less though.

Richard found himself being smothered by the patients as some of them stared at the new face. Finally he reached a bench near the window and sat down on the edge. For some reason the patients did not linger in this corner of the room. He took a deep breath and watched the room move as patients lost interest in some things and gained interest in others. A lot of them still liked the television.

When he turned to face the window in which the bench was facing, he saw the weather looked cold but inviting. There was a gentle breeze blowing through the trees. The fresh air was something he could do with at that moment. The rooms had become hot and sweaty with all the hustle and bustle of the patients and the mere volume of them.

In the corner of his eye he noticed someone was sat next to him. He hadn't realised she was there. He turned his head to see her clearer. Her hair was almost white and almost covered her face. She was wearing the uniformed shirt and trousers with a scruffy number on her sleeve. It was scruffier than the other ones he had seen on the patients and a slightly different colour fabric. "2.5.7?" he commented and smiled. She didn't stir; just staring out the window. He knew it was that same woman in the corridor, he was sure of it. His heart pounded, but awkwardly he tried again. “My name is Doctor Pearce.” He cleared his throat. “Do you remember me?” He placed his hands on his lap and swivelled his body to face her.

He was almost frightened when she moved. She caught his eye and he noticed her focus had veered to his left as if something was there. He turned. He could see nothing. As he smiled at her again, he noticed she was holding a piece paper against her lap. He tilted his head to see it and spoke again. “Is that a picture of the view?” he had kindness in his voice and he saw a glimmer of hope as he saw her almost smile. “May I see?”

The picture was of trees outside with three figures standing together. One figure had the same colour clothing as Matron, so Richard assumed it was her. The other two were a couple.

“Who are these?” Richard asked.

She pointed at one, which was the male and looked up at him.

“Me?” Richard thought it odd but continued to look at the picture. By the side of the trees and the three figures, was what looked like a lot of rubble. When he asked her about that, she opened another picture. This picture was of a bench with two people sat on it. Next to was another person slightly smaller than the others. There were no details within the drawing, just stick figures, like a child had drawn it. The paper looked quite old as well. The patient was around the same age as Richard, so he wondered if it was she drawn it or not.

He looked out of the window again and there was no one there. "Who is that?" he asked but she did not respond. "Did you draw this?"

She turned to look at him and for the first time they were facing each other. She opened her mouth to speak but Nurse Caddy had walked over to them. She had obviously been watching him at work. Richard felt her hand smooth his shoulder. He almost trembled. "I wouldn't bother a conversation with 2.5.7," she chuckled. Something had amused her.

"I've met her before I believe," Richard advised as he stood up from the bench. He noticed the patient had turned back to the window.

"That isn't possible, you know that right?" she explained, but his baffled expression made her explain further.

Richard felt it best not to mention their encounter. "What's your name?" He tried to prompt the patient's response.

"She doesn't have a *name* but a number; her room number. All our patients are numbered, it's just easier to remember them. Doctor De Ville did mention that to you didn't he? He is very specific with the rules."

Richard did not want to show his disagreement to her comments. He turned back to Patient 2.5.7 and hovered over her to see the picture she had drawn again. He noticed that one of the figures was wearing what looked like a white coat, similar to the ones some doctors' wear.

Caddy pulled him away. She introduced him to another patient, but his mind was solely on Patient 2.5.7. He returned to her like an invisible force drew him there. As he sat next to her again he carefully and gently took hold of the number on her arm. She twitched with anxiety and he moved away slightly.

Nurse Caddy came to his side again. "I can see what you're thinking Doctor Pearce."

"What do you mean?" Richard looked up at the pretty nurse.

"Richard don't choose this patient." She pushed him along a little so she could sit down.

"I don't mean to be rude Nurse Caddy but-"

"This patient is Doctor De Ville's and she has been in this hospital a long time."

"Is that why her arm band is warn compared with others?"

"Yes." Nurse Caddy had a serious expression. "See how the numbering is different, she has been here since she was a child, long before I started working here and these 'old' patients are untouchable. They are Doctor De Ville's and you don't want one of his."

Richard turned back to the patient he was sat near. She continued to stare into the abyss of the outside world within her own thoughts; if she had any. "I think I want to take that chance." He stood up and Caddy followed him. Then the patient spoke. Both he and Nurse Caddy turned around to see her.

"She wants to tell you something," she spoke with a quiet voice. It was a little croaky as she hardly spoke.

"Who?" Richard came a little closer.

Again Patient 2.5.7 looked to his left and he turned to look in the direction she had glanced to. He saw nothing. He asked her again and she just replied, "The little girl, Laurel." She turned back to the view and Richard was none the wiser. Who was the little girl?

When he and Nurse Caddy moved away, Nurse Caddy sighed with disbelief. "I've never seen that before," she commented.

"What?"

"She spoke to you."

"So?"

“She never speaks. Even when I’ve assisted with Doctor De Ville; she says nothing.”

“That is my answer then,” Richard nodded with reassurance of his thoughts.

“What?”

“My patient is Patient 2.5.7.” As he spoke he felt his need to know more about her and in fact she needed to know more about him. He needed to know who the little girl was that she had mentioned and he needed to understand why he was drawn to her so intensely.

When it came to returning to Doctor De Ville to notify him of his decision. Doctor De Ville groaned with acknowledgement. As he turned away from Richard he said one last thing, “Be careful with Patient 2.5.7, Doctor Pearce. If you are sure on your decision, do not get in my way.”

Chapter Five: Doctor De Ville 's Office

"Ah Pearce," Doctor De Ville acknowledged as he met Richard outside his office. "Come through. I have been thinking about your choice in patient and interested to find out your reasons behind your decision."

Richard followed him into the office that was quite dark. De Ville whipped the curtains open and sat behind his desk. Richard walked to the shelves of books, having a gander through them. There was an airless silence between them. Richard felt the urge to say something but instead created 'interested' grunts. He did not want to be the first one to speak.

"So Pearce," De Ville broke the silence sharply and Richard almost dropped the book he had been looking at.

"Yes sir?" he took a seat facing the desk.

"Why?"

"Why what? Oh sorry!" Richard realised what he had meant. "To be honest it was hard to choose," Richard began. "I saw her alone on one of the benches and felt she was the best candidate for my studies. I want to prove myself and she seems interesting."

"Hmm, prove is an interesting word in itself." De Ville paused lost within the verb. "I like that." He stood up from his seat and looked out the window. It needed a good clean. "You know you remind me of myself when I was just starting out. Was she your first choice? I mean there are a lot of them."

"Um, I did see a patient with extreme deformation, which I thought might be something I could get to grips with but I cannot give you an answer as to why I chose her, other than when she spoke, she-"

"Spoke!" Doctor De Ville gasped. "She spoke!? What did she say? What was her tone?" He rushed over to Richard and almost tugged at his collar but refrained. He took a breath and took a step back to gain some air. Richard pretended like he couldn't recall; he didn't want to say that he had a desire that he could not explain for her and Doctor De Ville frightened him. He had not seen the old man move so quickly or aggressively before. He must have touched a nerve.

Suddenly, a knock came from the door.

"Enter!" De Ville said firmly. He used the palm of his hand to tidy his grey hair over his balding scalp. He took another deep breath as if to compose himself and Richard saw Patient 2.5.7 come into the room with a porter, holding an end of piece of soft rope that was tied to the patient's wrist. "I decided to bring your choice for an introduction."

Richard felt his heart leap into his throat. He didn't understand why he felt so guilty choosing the patient.

There was something about her. Maybe that was why Doctor De Ville was being so protective.

Patient 2.5.7 looked tired. She dragged her feet behind her as she felt the tug of the rope. De Ville waved his hand and told the porter to remove the rope. When he did so, he was dismissed and the patient swayed with tiredness.

Richard shuffled in his chair uncomfortably as De Ville took a seat next to him. "So Pearce," De Ville leered at the patient. "Why this one?"

"I, I don't think I understand?" Richard pulled at his collar awkwardly.

"Well, she's one of mine and I want to know what brought you to her. You've said she was sat quietly on a bench. She's not the most conversational as you can see, but she spoke to you?"

"Well I suppose it is-"

"NO!" De Ville interrupted brashly and jumped up from his seat. Richard saw the patient flinch and her eyes had opened wide. "You have to be confident Pearce!"

"It was her eyes!" Richard spoke without hesitance but his erratic tone put a smile of De Ville's face. His wrinkles tightened with his smile. "I think she has something to say but just cannot say it."

"Good, Doctor Pearce, very good."

Richard sighed silently with relief and caught the patient's eyes again. He felt sorry for her. "She looks tired."

"Busy day Wednesdays. General tests to be done by me and its visitors' day of course."

"Who visits her?"

"That's the point; no one. We give her a double dose of the sedative to keep her mind off the fact no one cares for her." Richard saw the patient acknowledge what De Ville had said so carelessly.

"Doctor De Ville!"

"Oh don't worry, she doesn't understand what I'm saying."

"May I be present when you do the general tests next Wednesday?"

"No, I work alone when it comes to that sort of thing." De Ville responded abruptly. Richard could tell he was done with the conversation. "You can take Patient 2.5.7 back to her room so you can get acquainted."

"Yes Doctor De Ville," Richard replied. "And thank you." He stood up and walked towards her. She was shivering.

As De Ville sat back in his chair he swivelled to face the window he spoke again, "Oh and Pearce, use the rope.

Patient 2.5.7 doesn't like to be touched. It is easier this way and safer for you."

"Um, yes sir." Richard took hold of the end of the rope and gestured for her to go out the door first, which she did not understand. She stared at his hand that had gestured her, so he went first. As he shut the door behind the patient, he heard De Ville laugh to himself.

Richard cleared his throat. He breathed out the air he had be holding in the office.

They walked down the stairs in unison and the patient made sure she was one step behind him all the way. Richard found it disconcerting. Eventually he introduced himself as he had done before. "I'm Doctor Pearce from when I met you on the bench and I will be studying you for a while."

She didn't respond.

"I hope you will get used to the idea."

"Will you do the same as the other Doctor?"

"You mean Doctor De Ville? I suppose so; in a way." He saw her posture change as he answered her. She had crumpled slightly. He worried he had said something wrong. "We can see how we best work though isn't it?" he saw her tension ease so he tried to continue the flow of conversation. "You know Doctor De Ville seemed surprised you spoke to me. Do you have a reason for that?"

"I don't like to talk," she muttered.

"Could you tell me why?"

"I might say the wrong thing."

"You spoke to me though."

"Yes."

"Is it because you trust me more than the others or?" Richard hoped for the answer to be yes for some reason he didn't fully comprehend.

"I had to talk to you. The little girl was persistent." The patient did not look at him when she spoke, she continually looked at the ground. "She told me that you were the one."

"The one?"

"The one who will believe me."

"Who is the little girl?" Richard moved his hand to her arm but faltered as she flinched. As he moved away from her, he slipped on his next step and grabbed the first thing he could put his hands on the patient's arm.

He stabilised and in that same moment, saw a flash of something he didn't understand, but the image became clearer and morphed into a vision – like a moving film made privately in his mind.

There was a man aged between forty and fifty, dressed in a similar pyjama-like outfit that the patients wear, but more old fashioned. Richard thought it might even be as far back as the 1920s, judging by his hair. There was someone or something behind him. Richard couldn't quite see that far as it was blurred around the man.

Suddenly, with a flash of light, a whip came from the blurred figure and whipped the man sharp on the back. Richard's back stung like the skin had been ripped apart from the leather straps that must have been used. He heard the man scream with agony and blood dripped from the man's back slowly. Both he and Richard fell to their knees! Patient 2.5.7 came out of the mist that surrounded him. He blinked a few times and he had returned to the staircase still gripping the patient's shoulder. The pain was gone.

Richard took a few deep breaths and he trotted awkwardly with the patient until they reached the second floor, waiting for the door to be unlocked from the inside, by Nurse Gretel, who was on the night shift. Patient 2.5.7 had fallen silent again. They passed Nurse Gretel and Richard noticed her smile at him but on seeing the patient she took a few steps back. Richard found it strange. It was as if she didn't want to be touched by the patient. She was an odd woman, Richard thought. She had dyed blonde hair that could not have been brushed.

"Here we are then, room 2.5.7." It was locked. He peered down the corridor and Nurse Gretel giggled with her silliness of locking it. She tottered to them and unlocked the door.

"Be careful when you put her inside. You mustn't forget the rope," she said sternly. She rushed back to the desk at the end of the corridor by the staircase and Richard turned to the patient. She was already looking at him.

Although an awkward moment between them lingered, Richard couldn't help but feel something more that he didn't understand. The only way he could describe it was electricity, like a light has been turned on.

Then she did something he did not expect.

She offered the same gesture he had done when leaving De Ville's office. Richard took the offer and with a nod of his head entered her room. It made him smile. The room was small with a single bed and a chair and table. A window was barred and padlocked. Patient 2.5.7 brushed past him from behind and she climbed in her bed like a child, holding her knees to her chin.

"It's cold in here," Richard commented stepping next to the bed. He noticed the patient flinch as he had come closer to her, but as she did, he saw her grimace with pain. It was her back. "Can I see?"

Patient 2.5.7 lifted the back of her shirt and as he thought, there were whipping scars, like the man in his dream. "It is alright." He held his hands in the air defensively. When he saw her shoulder's relax, he picked up the very thin blanket at the bottom of the bed and gave it to her to keep her warm. "I'll see you soon for our first session. We can have another chat then."

He walked away from the bed and headed out of the room but he heard her breathe with a cold shiver. He looked back at her and she was still holding the blanket he had given her.

"Here, allow me," he said kindly and offered to take the blanket. With a nervous whimper she shakily gave it to him. "Lay back then." She listened to him and laid her head on the pillow. Richard carefully placed the blanket on top of her gently. After a moment of exchanging a look he went to the door. "Thank you," she whispered. Richard didn't turn back but smiled at the promise of conversation.

Chapter Six: January 1956 – The Case Study

I

On a Friday, the weather was very wet and murky. Richard rushed into his office with his trouser bottoms soaked and his coat dripping from the rain. He was late. The bus had been stuck in traffic. Mackenzie had already been in the office as his things had been thrown down. Richard threw off his coat and hat, then squeezed the water from his trouser bottoms. He took a deep breath after the run he had made from the bus stop. He shut his eyes for a moment to catch his breath but a light knock on the door interrupted him. Nurse Caddy appeared in the doorway. She had done her hair in a bun today.

"Matron has been looking for you," she said folding her arms and lifting her eyebrows. "You're late."

"I know, I know!" Richard squirmed as he tried tidying the papers Mackenzie had spread across their shared desk. "For goodness sake!" Papers fell onto the floor with Richard's frustration and both he and Nurse Caddy knelt to pick them up. Nurse Caddy had put more make up on than usual, Richard noticed. "Where is Matron?" he asked calmly.

"Just doing her rounds," she replied. "I wouldn't worry about the battle axe."

Richard smirked. "Do you say that to her face?"

"You're so funny," she joked and pushed him playfully. When they stood up together, Richard realised he was holding one paper with Nurse Caddy and he reached for her hand. She blushed as she released her grip. "Matron did put files on your desk about your patient."

"Well I suppose that must be what all these papers are?" Richard plonked them onto the desk again and shook his head but Nurse Caddy just giggled. "It's been a while to get these mind."

"Actually these papers are probably Doctor Mackenzie's because I moved yours to the shelves because I saw how Doctor Mackenzie came in this morning. He was worse than you!"

"You are lovely do you know that Nurse Caddy," Richard smiled and took both her hands, pulling her close.

"Call me Chloe. You better get on," she replied and pulled away from him. Once she had left Richard's sights, he found the file on the shelf. It was stamped with a doctor's name. He squinted to read it and of course, it read De Ville.

He pushed the random papers on the desk to one side to clear a space for his own and before he opened the file he studied the external. The edges were frayed and there were a number of pages that were not straight within the file. Richard assumed it was due to Doctor De Ville's significance to the detail. He felt his nerves bubble to the surface as he placed his thump on the bottom corner of the file to open.

He was unsure whether his nerves were due to the fact he had never had a proper patient to study before, or whether it was something about the patient herself. He still had nightmares of the man being whipped. He had had two meetings with the patient so far and she captured his attention so intensely that it lingered within the mind for a couple hours of leaving her. He thought about her innocently sitting on her bed as he tucked her in.

On opening the file carefully so not to lose any loose papers, he saw a number of drawings that looked like they had been done by a child. It was similar to the one that the patient had been holding when he first introduced himself to her. All the pictures were of a setting, whether it be fields and trees or within a house. But in every picture there was some figure. He was unsure whether it was the same figure in every picture or just the drawings were the same. Richard realised after flicking through a number of the pictures that at some point they were all stapled together. He looked a little harder; and noticed that there must be some pictures missing because there were scuffs of paper around the staple that was left.

In the end, he decided it was best to move on within the file where there were notes and dates of sessions Doctor De Ville had made progress with the patient. All the notions seemed to be heading in the same direction, Schizophrenia. A lot of the pages looked old and when Richard found the earliest dated, he realised that Patient 2.5.7 had been in the hospital for quite a number of years and the reason there were child drawings within the file was that she was a child when she first arrived. "Twenty one years?!" he gasped as he flicked from the first page in the file to check the date of birth and then to the page he was on. She was twenty seven now. "Her whole life stuck in this place?" he muttered catching his breath as he said it.

"A long time," said a voice at the door suddenly.

"Matron!" Richard stood up from behind his desk as he saw Matron standing in the doorway.

"I assume you are looking into Doctor De Ville's file," she said with an assertive tone. "I am surprised Doctor De Ville allowed you one of his patients at all but 2.5.7 is even more honourable."

"Why more so in regards to Patient 2.5.7?"

"Shouldn't you be getting on?" she turned briskly and waited for him outside the office. He followed her gesture with the file in his hand. He was bewildered by the secrecy on 2.5.7 and wanted to push the matter, but

Matron was the wrong person to ask. He was going to have to ask Nurse Caddy.

He walked with Matron to room 2.5.7, swinging his case beside him slightly like he had a tune in his mind. Matron gave him a stern look and he followed her quietly. The nurse on duty on the second floor was Nurse Caddy, which Richard could not hide his smile for seeing her. She glanced up at him from the small table she was sitting at and stood up as Matron began to speak. "The nurse on duty always has the charge of the keys," Matron stated, holding out her palm for Nurse Caddy to give her the correct key. "Come with me." Matron's footsteps were echoed as she powered down the corridor. She stopped at the room and waited for Richard to catch up, rolling her eyes as he smiled apologetically. The old lock turned with a crank and a click as Matron stiffly used the key. Richard couldn't help but peek back at Nurse Caddy, but from where room 2.5.7 was situated compared to her table at the end of the corridor, he could only just see her arm. He found it strange how the corridors were not straight. "I shall leave you to it then Doctor Pearce."

"Oh thank you Matron," Richard replied with a slight startled tone as he had been leaning back to get a better view of Nurse Caddy. Matron did not voice her disapproval of his behaviour.

When her footsteps had dimmed enough, Richard took a deep breath and opened the door. He felt he should have knocked as he saw Patient 2.5.7 jump as he came into sight.

As he was about to take his first step inside, Nurse Caddy had tapped him on the shoulder. She handed him the rope in with to tie the patient with if needed and then gestured for him to go inside.

Patient 2.5.7 had lost interest in him by the time he entered. She was staring at one of the corners of the room. He cleared his throat to try and grab her attention but again, not even a look in his direction.

"I'm sorry to disturb you," he commented while shutting the door.

Suddenly she jumped as he spoke like she had believed it to be someone else. When she turned to him, the fear in her eyes startled him. "Do you not remember me? Doctor Pearce?"

She nodded at him in response.

"Are you alright me being in your room?" He wondered about where he would sit but she stood from her chair that she had been sitting on and placed it slightly further away from the bed. With a pause to look at his complexion again, she then scrambled onto the bed in the corner against the wall.

Richard sat down slowly. He saw how she held onto herself was child-like. He decided to be silent for a while and see what she might do or say. This time she was wearing a long greyish white nightgown, still with the band around her arm. He was fascinated with the arm band. He noticed how the sleeve of the nightgown had be cut or rather ripped in order to still show the arm band. It was always in the right place unlike her other garment that did not fit right. Only a square piece had been cut out. It was a strange way of doing it. *Maybe she didn't want to take it off,* he thought.

She tilted her head and then turned to her arm bad, placing her hand over it as if he had said his thoughts out loud. There were bags under her eyes; she obviously did not sleep that well.

"May I take a photograph of you? For an update; for your file?" Richard asked opening his case he had placed beside him. He took out a camera and gestured for her to smile.

She sat up a little but did not smile. The flash of the camera stunned her slightly and she blinked a couple of times to gain her focus.

As he put the camera away, there was a long awkward silence.

Finally he felt he needed to say something to break the lingered silence within the room, but she stopped him. He had opened his mouth to speak she held up her hand.

"Where is the other doctor?" she spoke with a woman's voice yet her tone was like that of an inquisitive child's.

"Doctor De Ville? He's allowing me to help. Do you remember our previous conversation?" Richard was unsure what to say. He felt it best to start asking questions. Although he had been studying psychology for years, he had never had any field work, so he was unsure of himself and for some reason she put him even more uneasy than any other patient he had come across in the asylum so far. Patient 2.5.7's whole persona screamed mystery to him that he needed to find out what was concealed. "Do you know why you are here?"

Patient 2.5.7 had heard this many a time and her expression of hopefulness had sunken to a sameness state. "Of course. Do you?"

"I ask the questions."

"You have not asked many worth answering."

"Well you have not fully answered my first question. Why are you here?" He did not like being challenged but there was a knowingness in her voice that made it seem like she knew this.

“I answered your first question. This one is your second. I am here because I have always been here. I am here because it is meant to be.”

“Do you understand what this place is?”

“Yes.” Her eyes narrowed knowing his next question, and Richard moved his chair closer to her. “It is called a hospital for the illnesses that are in their minds.”

“I like that answer.” Richard smiled kindly and he noticed her concentration alter to something behind him. He twisted his upper body. There was nothing that he could see. “What do you see?”

She didn’t reply so he asked again.

No answer.

When he turned back to her, he saw how her whole body language had changed. It reminded him of when he was sat next to her on the bench in the communal room.

“Patient 2.5.7, are you alright?”

“Are you alone in this world doctor?” she asked with her eyes only moving to acknowledge him.

“I have a mother.” He hesitated. *Do I ask her the same question,* he pondered.

“My mother left me here; and my father” she stated, which took him aback. He did not expect her to open up, but she was still looking at something behind him.

"That must have been awful."

"I remember that they wouldn't even say goodbye when the doctor took me to my room." She leaned forward a little beginning to get used to his presence. Richard was within touching distance of her now and he resisted the urge to take her hand. "May I ask you something Doctor?" she spoke again looking up at him kindly.

As he looked into her eyes, he realised her eyes were different colours. One was a very light blue and the other was a very light green. "Of course you can," he struggled to complete his sentence as he wanted to name her.

"You mentioned about your mother," her voice lowered a little. "What about your sister?"

Richard's right eyebrow rose with confusion, "No? I am an only child." He thought it strange the way she asked. Why not brother? Why not sibling? The patient began looking at his left side again, like someone was there. "Who do you see?" Richard asked and leaned forward to try and touch her.

Patient 2.5.7 flinched and backed away.

"It's alright," he whispered. "I promise." He moved onto the bed with her and offered his hand. Like a frightened but intrigued rabbit she crept closer to him. She moved her arm in line with his and straightened her wrist slowly so her hand was in line as well.

"I don't want to hurt you."

"Who do you see?" he asked again. Their eyes met and he saw her trembling cease and the trust he was forming with her.

Finally he gently touched the tips of her fingers with hers. He felt a spark; like electricity or static within the nerves of his hand.

Suddenly a wooziness came over him. He blinked a couple of times to clear his focus. He took her hand gently and the spark he had felt turned to a painful sting that ran up his left arm. He let out a whimper by the shock of the pain and when he looked at Patient 2.5.7, he saw she was no longer looking at him. She was looking at something in the corner of the room. Richard followed her gaze.

His mouth dropped and his eyes widened. He saw a little girl standing sopping wet with water droplets forming a puddle around her. Her clothes were dated and she had lost one shoe somewhere. When the little girl realised he could see her, she smiled and made a gentle wave. He heard whispers of a name he couldn't quite catch.

Suddenly there was a knock at the door and patient 2.5.7 leapt into the air like a frightened mouse. She clung to her very thin pillow. Richard also jumped up from the bed.

Matron entered. "Why is the door shut?" she asked.

Richard stood still awkwardly. "I," he paused to think of an excuse. "I didn't realise there was a rule about doors."

"Alone in a bedroom with a patient," she patronised him with a raised voice. As he stepped towards her to apologise, he saw in the corner of his eye, Patient 2.5.7 had begun rocking back and fore. Matron lectured him of the importance of safety but her voice trailed away when she heard the patient murmuring.

"Matty," the patient muttered. When both Richard and Matron looked in her direction, she continued to rock back and fore, staring at her bed.

"Patient?" Matron muttered.

As she rocked, she chanted. "Matty the fatty doesn't like to play-"

"What??"

"-Matty the fatty that's all they say."

Matron moved passed Richard and into the room, stepping slowly like the floor could crumble at any moment. "W-w-what did you say?" she stuttered.

"Matty the fatty doesn't like to play. Matty the fatty that's all they say," she repeated and then began to say it quicker and louder like a spell. "Matty the fatty doesn't like to play. Matty the fatty that's all they say!"

Matron stumbled backwards and into Richard that shook her; she almost screamed. Richard tried to console her but she ran out of the room and down the corridor. She shoved Nurse Caddy out of the way, who fell onto the floor on impact.

Richard rushed to her side and assisted her to her feet. "Are you alright?" he asked gripping her tightly. She nodded with her mouth partially open and pressed her hand on the back of her head. She had knocked it against the wall. Both she and Richard turned back to room 2.5.7, where the door was still open.

Richard took the first step towards the room. Inside, Patient 2.5.7 was in the same seated position as she had been and that little girl in the corner had gone. He had heard what Patient 2.5.7 had been chanting but it meant nothing to him. The pruned complexion of the little girl haunted him.

"Do you know what she meant?" he asked Nurse Caddy.

"Matron's name is Matilda," she said gravely. She signalled to Richard for them to leave. And catching his concern at leaving the patient in this state but she reassured him she would be ok before locking the door behind them.

As they walked back to her table at the end of the corridor, she explained how strange things happen when

Patient 2.5.7 is around. “She knows things,” she explained.

“What things? How?”

“That’s just it; none of us know, but we just keep our distance and Doctor De Ville looks after her. If she has an episode like many patients do then we call Doctor De Ville. He’s the only doctor on sight in the night time anyway.”

“He sleeps here?” Richard leaned against the wall with his arms folded as Nurse Caddy sat in her chair.

“Yes in his office. The others do the same as you; shift work.” Nurse Caddy noticed Richard’s chuckle as she said that so questioned him.

“At the moment I haven’t really got a place,” Richard explained that his rent had increased and he was struggling to pay it as well as commute to the asylum every day. He was hoping to find a place nearby but there was nothing available so had been sleeping in his office every other night to catch up on work and sleep.

Eventually, they said goodnight and Richard caught the last bus home. Nurse Caddy had explained that she could tell him stories about 2.5.7 but it wasn’t safe to talk about within the asylum. They agreed to discuss it another time.

Matron did not return to work for a couple of days and when she finally did show herself, she said nothing of the night, although all the nurses had been filled in on what had happened. The strange thing that occurred to Richard was that none of them seemed surprised that it was Patient 2.5.7 who had put her uneasy. Everyone seemed to know something he didn't and he needed to speak with Nurse Caddy about it.

There was something altogether strange about the patient, that Richard was desperate to find out the source.

II

Richard sat in the darkness of his bedroom waiting for a phone call. Lost in thought about the strange occurrence between Patient 2.5.7 and Matron, the telephone finally rang and he picked it up instantly with a tired sounding hello. It was his mother. She rambled on about the gossip in the village where he was from. It was mainly moaning about people Richard had distant memories of. It always comforted him to hear her ranting and stressing about something as it meant she was fine. She was happy. It was just the way she was.

"And how is your patients? Still nuts?" Richard heard her ask; she was joking of course.

"Mum,-"

"I know! Wrong terminology and all that but seriously how is everything? Are you eating properly? Sleeping? And are you making those patients well again?"

"Yes Mum. It's just harder than I thought it was going to be. I have only been assigned one patient and that tires me out so I am not looking forward to taking on more."

"Why is that?"

"I don't know. It just feels strange in this place?

"Do you want to come home?" there was an element of hope within her voice. Her son back at home; safe.

"No no I'm fine Mum. I just need to go to bed that is all and find somewhere closer to work. Same time next week?"

"Ok my darling, look after yourself, take care and maybe I could come up and visit you or something. Once you've settled in?"

"That sounds nice to me."

"Love you."

"Yes Mum. Love you too. Goodnight."

He put the telephone back on its receiver and slumped back into his chair. With his eyes closed for a moment, he heard a rustle. Opening his eyes he saw the little girl, who was soaking wet, missing a shoe. He jumped out of his eat. Not even being able to scream. Her hair was draped over her face so it was hard to see her face. She raised her arm and pointed to his satchel. When he looked at it and then back to her, she was gone.

Within his satchel he pulled out the file of Patient 2.5.7. He was told not to take official documents from the hospital but he had not placed it there. It was so large and detailed.

He removed the pictures that the patient had drawn over the years and noticed in some, was the same little girl. He looked at the facts from Doctor De Ville's notes. He saw a trend that every Wednesday meeting had no notes. They had been removed. It just had the date, if the session was completed and how long it was. As he had read before, most of the details were based on the illness, Schizophrenia, but later in De Ville's notes he writes about paranoia.

Someone is there; someone is always there; you cannot hide from them; they know; she knows; you know.

This quote was written quite a few times within Doctor De Ville's notes and the more Richard read the scribbles, the more it felt like De Ville was writing his own personal feelings than the patient's. Richard also noted how De Ville's handwriting had become a lot more squiggly and untidy as he got older, but more importantly Wednesday was always his worst day. He found another figure that Patient 2.5.7 had mentioned within De Ville's notes. It is a woman, pale and a similar schizophrenia tendencies as Richard's patient. She was darker and older however. Out of the description, Richard found scraps of papers Patient 2.5.7 had drawn the woman.

The eerie scribbling of the dark figure gradually got worst the later the drawings were dated. Finally, Richard found a drawing that gave more details. It was only of the eye, but the eye had blood smudged around the iris. The drawing gave Richard the shivers, so he decided it was time to put the file away.

The clock struck midnight so Richard threw the file onto his armchair near his bed and climbed into bed sluggishly. He reached for the side lamp to turn it off but noticed one of the pictures had fallen on the floor. Crawling to the end of the bed and picked it up. It was a similar one to the one he saw with the patient. A man and a woman sitting on a bench in front of a window and a little girl near them. On this one there was a small note written in a little girl's hand writing that read: *he will believe me.* He placed this picture in his jacket pocket. He knew it was important.

It wasn't until he reached the asylum again, that he remembered the picture. He saw Nurse Caddy walking a patient to a room, and caught up to her. "I need to speak with you," he said briskly, still holding the picture in his hand.

Richard tried to be careful as he spoke in front of the patient Nurse Caddy was guiding. He sensed Nurse Caddy's nervousness as he tried to show her the drawing. "I am thinking that this is her and that is me," he said pointing at the drawings.

"Nope you are definitely wrong there," said the patient with a high squeaky voice.

Richard looked at her for the first time as she spoke. Her hair was dyed and brushed well. She had amended her night gown differently than the other patients in order to highlight her figure. "SSHH 1.2.1!" Nurse Caddy growled and yanked her violently.

"No, No Chloe, Let her speak," Richard spoke calmly and they halted in one of the communal rooms.

"Chloe aye?" Patient 1.2.1 cackled in a teasing tone and winked. "That's a drawing by that mad one ain't it?"

"Patient-" Chloe began but 1.2.1 interrupted.

"Call me Lucinda! My Name! Lu-Cin-Da! UGH!" she threw herself to the floor and sat cross legged, thumping her fists on the hard green tiled floor.

"Lucinda," Richard said kindly and crouched down beside her. He took her hands to stop her from hitting them. "What did you mean?"

"Have you touched her like that?" she asked with a menacing undertone.

Richard faltered, he didn't know how to react to the question. He released her hands and shuffled away from her slightly. "W-who?"

"2.5.7 of course," she chuckled. "That is one of hers. You pointed at the little girl when you said you believed it was her; that is wrong. The little girl is her imaginary friend." She paused and swiped the drawing from Richard's hands. "But it's strange." She stared at the picture.

"How so?" Richard asked and joined her study of the picture. Nurse Caddy was still standing. It was obvious she was concerned that Matron could come in at any moment.

"The little girl is only around when no one else is with her, yet there is a man in this picture also. And if that is you, well," she breathed. "You're an important fella!" She gave the drawing back to him, still with a bewildered expression upon her face. She stood up and turned to Nurse Caddy to take her away.

Richard also stood but stayed in the same spot. As Nurse Caddy walked with Patient 1.2.1, nearing the door. Richard called to them. “What did you mean when you asked me if I had touched her in that way, Lucinda?”

“Why don’t you try it and see what happens?” she called back and cackled madly. “Or if you’re scared you can always ask Enid!” The door slammed as the left the room and Lucinda’s last words echoed in his mind. He had never heard of Enid? Was she the little girl? Was she another imaginary fixation? Or was she someone important? Lucinda’s laughter haunted his mind also. It was like she knew something that he didn’t know himself. He felt him losing any sense he had before entering the asylum to the patients of Gravehill Asylum.

He stayed in the same communal room and waited for Nurse Caddy to return. He knew she would not let him down. When she did return, she moved secretively and her expression on her face was very shady. He did not question it as he was too overwhelmed with the intrigue of Enid.

He asked. She replied with little information – only to meet her after dark at the Nurses’ House, which was across the yard from the asylum within the grounds.

As soon as it became dark outside, Richard looked out for Matron. There was no sign of her. He moved swiftly across the yard and as he breathed he could see his breath mist in front of his face. He reached the Nurses' sleeping quarters and noticed the front door had been left ajar for him. Nurse Caddy was waiting for him just inside the entrance. She was wearing a normal every day dress, with her hair curled. When he reached her, the door for the gate keeper's hut creaked open and the old man peered his head around the door. Nurse Caddy grabbed Richard fiercely by the trim of his blazer and pulled him out of sight. The old gatekeeper had looked in the direction of the Nurses' House and looking in judgement with a cold expression. Nurse Caddy watched through the clouded glass on the main front door until the gatekeeper disappeared back into his hut.

Richard straightened himself and took a deep breath of release. As he opened his mouth to speak, Nurse Caddy thrust herself towards him and kissed him passionately on the lips. She tugged at his hair on the back of his head and with the force, Richard fell back against the wall. He placed his hands on Chloe's back and kissed her back.

When she withdrew herself, she took Richard's hand and led him up the lift, where she paused outside a room. "You know you said that you were struggling to commute here and back again to you apartment?"

Richard recalled the short conversation he had had with her a while ago now and nodded in response. With his gesture of acknowledgement, she opened the door revealing her bedroom. “I have a spare bed.” she went inside and Richard hesitantly followed.

“I cannot stay here Chloe,” Richard chose his words wisely. “The other nurses will know! And if Matron found out-”

“They don’t need to find out Rick!” she said pulling him closer to her. “The nurses including me are not close. We keep to ourselves. Its best that way.” Her voice had saddened like something had reminded her of an upsetting time. “We learnt the hard way.”

“Who used to share with you then?” Richard enquired as he saw a few things around that were on the side of the spare bed.

“Another nurse,” she replied solemnly. “She; she doesn’t work here anymore.”

Richard sat on what could be his bed and looked at her caringly. She smiled and sat next to him. “I must tell you something before you meet Enid,” she began. Richard took her hand in his to console her. “Enid is a retired nurse who was really close to your Patient 2.5.7. And so was my roommate; my friend. Things happen when you get too involved with patients Rick and you’ll see that when you meet Enid.”

“I understand,” Richard responded in a typical doctor tone. “May I meet her?”

"One more thing," Chloe stood and headed to the door where Richard followed. "She may not have the answers to your questions as she gets very confused. And she forgets a lot of things these days."

"I understand," Richard whispered and kissed Chloe gently.

He was then taken to Enid's room. He knocked lightly on the door. When they entered, Richard noticed the room was minimal with a bed and a wardrobe. It reminded him of the patient rooms, just with more colour. The old nurse was sat in a rocking chair by the window. Her hair was grey and her skin was leathery. The moonlight glimmered onto her complexion.

She smiled as they came and sat near her. "Now don't you make a lovely couple?" she croaked in her old shaky voice.

Richard chuckled awkwardly and replied, "We're not a couple." He cleared his throat with a glance in Chloe's direction.

"That is indeed a shame." She turned away and looked out the window again.

"Enid??" Richard tried to get her attention.

"I was hoping you could help me with a patient of mine."

"I have looked after a lot of patients during my career, but it was a long time ago since I have."

"Well you have dealt with this particular patient before," Richard rubbed the back of his neck. He felt uncomfortable asking.

"Well that was probably some time ago so I may disappoint."

"Definitely not Enid," Chloe reassured her.

"Ah Chloe my dear, he's a keeper here isn't he," she smiled innocently.

Richard also felt reassured by Chloe and tried to ignore Enid's personal remarks about them. He continued. "You probably don't remember a female patient, um, 2.5.7?"

She stirred and her pupils expanded as her rocking chair froze in mid swing. "Numbers."

"Pardon Enid?"

"She never liked her numbers." Her bottom lip quivered. "She always said they were bad numbers. The previous 2.5.7 was bad very bad." She did not look at Richard as she spoke and continued to stare out the window onto the starry sky.

"So you do remember her?"

"So many memories in one mind." She continued to stare into nothing, looking past both Richard and Nurse Caddy as they tried to grab her attention.

"I don't understand?" Richard leaned to her.

"I think she might be having one of her episodes," Nurse Caddy whispered. "We should go." She moved away, but as Richard followed her, Enid clutched his arm with a pinch.

He turned back. "Are you the man who is going to help her? She is waiting. Waiting for that person to believe. I never believed but now you're here!"

"What?"

"Patient 2.5.7 knows things you did not want her to know. But she is scared just as scared as you are; she was just as scared as I was." Enid clung to Richard's arm like a bird's claw. Richard was lost within her dark eyes.

"2.5.7?"

"Don't say the numbers! Evil numbers!" she tightened her grip of his arm. "Find her name Doctor! Find her name and help her!"

"I don't understand Enid?" Richard managed to pull her claw-like grip from his arm. He had puncture wounds from her nails.

"I still talk to her you know." Her voice had softened

"You mean you visit her." Richard came closer to her again. Chloe shrugged and shook her head.

"I see her and she sees me but both of us are not really there. She doesn't see all of me – not the old me. She sees me of what I once was."

"Rick, Doctor Pearce, I think we'd better leave it for now," Chloe interrupted who was standing by the door.

"So much guilt," she squealed as they headed to the door.

Richard stopped and pulled away from Nurse Caddy who had hold of his hand. He didn't have to say anything.

"Tell her I'm sorry!"

"Sorry for what?"

She burst into tears and wailed as if in pain. "I helped him! I always helped him! No matter how cruel! The room is dark and metallic. The room is dark and grim. So much blood!"

"Enid, what room?"

"Basement is where he takes her. And basement is where he always used to take her. Pain and cruelty and pain"

"Richard we need to leave her now!" Chloe tugged him harshly. "She's ill and I think she's said enough."

"But I don't understand what she means," Richard had turned his back on Enid. Chloe gave him a stern look to leave the room, but suddenly Richard felt a sharp sting in his back.

He swivelled round and Enid's frail body had crept behind him. As he looked down at her wrinkled face, she had tears in her eyes. Finally she muttered one more thing to Richard before pushing her hand against his chest, "tell her I am sorry. Hold her and you will see; you will understand." Richard felt the stinging sensation move to his chest as she pushed harder. Although she was frail, her strength seemed supernatural and as the stinging intensified everything fell into darkness.

Suddenly Richard was absorbed in flashes of events that he was unaware of the place and of the time they stood. In a putrid green tiled room, Richard saw blurred figures hovering over a metal contraption. There was a child inside. Richard tried to move closer but he could only move with a young Nurse Enid Brookes.

He felt her look down at the child, who had tears in her eyes and the leather straps bruised her skin around her forehead, arms and legs. He heard her cry "please not again I won't tell anymore" and although Richard felt the nurse hesitate, the doctor commanded her to put a mouth piece in the little girl's mouth. A zapping sound from the power generator echoed through the room and the little girl was electrocuted, shaking by the force of it. Richard had turned away from the sight and caught the face of the doctor. Even though it was blurred and murky, his shining white teeth that had created the grin on his face, revolted Richard so much that he felt a gagging sensation. So much so, that the vision began to break apart like an old film reel that had been damaged. That face he had seen before. That face, although older now, had stayed the same. That face was Doctor De Ville's.

Richard's eyes flickered open. They were bloodshot and sore. He felt sick. When he looked around, he appeared to be in Chloe's bedroom again, with the two single beds and the two wardrobes. He turned to his left and saw Chloe sitting beside him on the other bed. He had been tucked into a bed and a damp towel rested on his forehead.

"Nurse Caddy-" he croaked.

"Don't try and speak," she interrupted, removing the towel. "And call me Chloe, there is no one else here."

He smiled and sat up. "What happened?"

"You fainted. It was the strangest of things."

Richard tried to think of what he had dreamed but it had gone from his mind. "I should leave."

"No rest a while. You need to. I thought about calling for a doctor if you weren't going to wake in the next hour. I was concerned."

"Really?" Richard smiled. Then he remembered Enid. "Enid said a few things."

"I know she did." Chloe held herself tightly, containing her guilt. "Look Rick. I haven't been fully up front with you."

"Go on." Richard sat up.

"There have been a few occasions with Patient 2.5.7 that are creepy; the things she knows. My roommate may not be working here. But she hasn't left."

"Really? Then we must talk to her."

"That's just it. She is a patient now. In the intensive ward. And Patient 2.5.7 put her there."

"What's the intensive ward?"

"The ward that patients are taken to if they become violent. They're not supposed to be there full time, but she can't come out."

"How did Patient 2.5.7 put her there?"

"She touched her; making her see things that weren't really there."

"That is impossible you and I both know that." But he believed her.

"I know the medical understanding but you didn't see the change in her when she began assisting Doctor De Ville with his patients."

"Is it Doctor De Ville rather than the patient then?"

"No. Doctor De Ville has one patient left from that era. Some have died and others moved on but Patient 2.5.7 has a special place with him and I think that is because she makes other people ill too." Chloe was dead serious about what she was saying and Richard found it hard to comprehend.

"Chloe, where is the intensive ward? And what is her name?"

"It's passed the communal rooms and locked by a nurse and guard 24 hours a day. Her name was Pamela. But I don't know if that is still her inside.

Richard excused himself from her room. Chloe tried to slow him down as she did not want him going in there too hyped. He could tell Chloe did not seem impressed with him going so soon, but he gave her a gentle kiss on the cheek. As he walked along the gravel to the hospital he remembered the comments Nurse Enid Brookes had made. He looked up at her window from the distance he had walked and she was already staring back at him. She nodded with acknowledgement as he saw her. She then disappeared like a ghost from behind her curtain. Patient 2.5.7 had taken over his thoughts.

III

Matron was sat in reception when Richard rushed in. She looked up in surprise at seeing him back so late in the evening. He hardly glanced in her direction as he passed her. Running through the number of communal rooms and reached a door he had not entered before. He stopped for a moment and panted. He pushed the door open, entering the kitchen. There were no cooks there at this time of night. It was dark and still had dirty dishes in the sink. There was a horrible odour the further he went inside. He followed the odour to the walk in refrigerator. He reached out towards the handle on the door.

Suddenly Matron and Nurse Caddy rushed in! The door had created a loud bang which echoed through the empty rooms on the ground floor of the building. "Doctor Pearce!" Matron exclaimed. "What on earth are you doing?"

"I," he thought for a moment trying to think of an excuse. "I am looking for the intensive ward. Where is it?"

"Well it's not in the refrigerator Doctor Pearce!" Matron took a step from the doorway and gestured for him to leave. Nurse Caddy followed her gesture immediately like a well-trained dog.

Frustrated, he marched out of the kitchen and looked at Nurse Caddy angrily. He noticed her eyes flit further down the corridor. He knew that was where the intensive ward was. He moved quickly and could hear the shouts from Matron as he hurried away.

"You do not have clearance to visit any of the patients in this ward!"

Richard reached the intensive ward location. He stopped in front of the iron barred gate that was the entrance of the ward. It had a sign next to it stating that only certain limited personnel had access to this ward.

A nurse, who was behind the gate stood up in shock that someone was there. Richard had not seen this nurse before and he had been working for the asylum for almost a year now. He straightened his tie and wiped the beads of sweat from his forehead. He asked if he could be let in, but the nurse did not respond she just looked at him vacantly. Footsteps were coming closer and Matron, with Nurse Caddy, reached him.

"Doctor De Ville is coming. It is his decision on who enters this ward. You need to wait for him." She explained calmly.

Richard, too impatient to wait, demanded her to open the gate, so Matron did so. He reminded her of the encounter with Patient 2.5.7 and how this could explain some mysteries. Her usual stern expression, changed to nervousness. The only other time he had seen her that way was when Patient 2.5.7 spoke to her. He must have touched a nerve.

The locked ward looked newer than the rest of the hospital as Richard stepped inside, but that was only because it was hardly used. Eerily clean. He heard the lock of the door behind him, where the nurse who was on duty stood and watched him; and Matron and Nurse Caddy stayed on the other side of the gate with their hands clenching the metal bars. Richard returned to his slow walk through the corridor. It seemed thinner than the others. The floor squeaked as he made his way through. He felt his heart thump in his chest as he listened to every step he made. A tap and then a squeak; a tap and a squeak were the only noises he could here. The corridor was walled with tiles unlike the rest of the hospital that were white while the floored tiles were the horrible green colour. He reached the four doors at the end. Three of the rooms were empty, but the fourth contained the nurse. These doors were heavy; heavier than the normal bedroom doors.

He took a deep breath and opened the hatch on the door to see inside. At first he could only see the room. It was padded with foam-like pillows all around the walls.

Suddenly, there was a bang. The patient sniggered. Then he saw her. Her greasy black hair was draped over her face as she swung from side to side putting weight of each foot separately. Her arms were tied with rope to the ceiling of the room and then her ankles where chained to the floor. "Who are you?" she said still giggling.

"Doctor Pearce, I was hoping to pick your brains about a patient of mine." He tried to hide his nervousness but her whole demeanour frightened him.

"I am honoured! Which one?"

"May I ask your name first?"

"It's Pamela," she said with an almost disgusted tone. "I wasn't given a number. What number did you want to talk about?"

"Patient," he hesitated. "Two-"

"Five?" she questioned and she knew by Richard's perturbed face that she was right so she continued, "Seven."

"Yes," he leaned in closer. "You remember her then?" His eyes squinted with intrigue.

She threw herself to the door and he smelt her stale breath. Her arms were stretched back by the rope. "Don't let her touch you! Don't let her touch you!" she chanted and whispered.

"Why not?" he spoke over her.

"If you do, you will end up like me."

"I don't understand? How can a woman make you like this?"

"She sees things, things that we can't see. Things we cannot comprehend!"

"Like what?"

"Death."

“What?” Richard pulled at his collar.

“I shouldn’t had touched her! She showed me w-w-what she sees. The death; the decay; the pain!” she screamed in agony and dropped to the floor.

“Stop! Stop!” he tried to calm her down.

She stood up suddenly and Richard took a step back, but stayed in view. “He’s coming. I can smell him.”

“Who?”

“Go to the basement and you will understand. It was his fault! He made me help him! But these people NEVER LISTEN! They JUST JUDGE!” she screamed her last words with an agonising wail, before whispering, “Go inside and see what secrets it hides.” She said these words so quickly that Richard thought he might have misheard.

“There’s a basement?” Richard tried to get some sense from her riddles.

“I used to go to the basement. He trusted me. He trusted me with his secrets. TERRIBLE! Terrible things in the basement. Unforgivable things in the basement. Don’t let him pick you to go there. The others will not forget you then! 2.5.7 will not forget that you went there!” She spoke quickly.

Richard moved closer again. He tried to speak but his voice was lost by someone calling him. “Pearce!” the voice bellowed. Richard jumped after hearing his name from behind him. It was Doctor De Ville. "Is she saying anything?" He demanded to know with an essence of urgency in his throat.

"Nothing that is coherent sir." Richard lied.

"That is expected. I wish you had waited for me."

"Sorry, I just wanted to find some information."

"About Patient 2.5.7?"

"Yes."

"Hmm, it is not surprising your studies led you to this unfortunate creature. She became obsessed." He met Richard at the door and slammed the peep hole shut, blocking out the screams of foul language by the patient. De Ville was wearing his pyjamas with a badly made tie over the top of his fancy dressing gown, like he had made some sort of effort to look dressed. He walked with Richard back through the corridor with his hands behind his back as he walked. "I would stay away from her in future."

"Yes sir."

Matron had been stood at the locked door waiting for them and locked the door after they had withdrawn from the ward. Richard caught her eye and realised that she was hiding something. Something she was feeling guilty for. He looked to Nurse Caddy who was still there in her normal clothes with a worried expression. De Ville acknowledged both of the women and as he walked passed Nurse Caddy commented on her dress. “Here after hours I see Nurse. I want you to come to my office tomorrow morning. When does your shift start?”

“Um, seven thirty, Doctor De Ville.” Her voice was croaky.

“Good come straight up then. And Matron you to be there at seven am. I will return to my quarters now and Doctor Pearce,” he spun on one foot with a squeak, very spritely for an old man. “Do not disobey my rules again please. Especially when it involves one of my patients.”

“Yes sir. Sorry sir.” Richard nodded quickly and he watched as De Ville and Matron walked back through the communal rooms towards reception. She turned back with a knowing glance at Richard and Nurse Caddy, which made Richard feel petrified at what he had unearthed. His next step was going to be a challenge. He was to visit 2.5.7 again.

He returned with Nurse Caddy to the Nurses’ House without the others knowing and he spent the night in her room. He apologised to her for getting her into trouble but she didn’t mind. She wasn’t looking forward to her meeting with De Ville though, Richard was more worried about his own meeting he was going to have the next day; with Patient 2.5.7.

IV

Richard had waited a few weeks before seeing Patient 2.5.7 again. He had processed the conversations he had had with the number of people who had been involved with the patient. He had been secretly living with Chloe for a while now so needed to wait until the nurses on the early shifts had walked over to the asylum.

When he arrived at the reception, he passed Matron who commented on his booking of consultation room. He chose to ignore her and continued to his office preparing notes. A nurse came over to him and handed him an envelope. He thanked her and when he opened it, he remembered he had asked for the photograph to be developed. The photo was of Patient 2.5.7 sitting on her bed, no smile on her face. The photo was quite clear, but a blur surrounded the patient. Richard had not seen anything like that in a photograph before. He took out a magnifying glass from the top desk drawer and focused on the blurring in the photo. When he looked carefully, it looked like distorted images of faces. He put the photo away in horror. It was scary to look at it. The distorted image around the patient seemed to be prodding and poking her constantly, which Richard believed could be the reason why the patient had scratch marks and bruises on her arms.

The time for his session with his patient came quite quickly. He waited for her to be brought by one of the nurses. It was one of the first times he had been in one of the consultation rooms. They were similar to the doctors' offices that were also on the top floor. It was a nice change from seeing the cold tiles that were on the walls and floor because instead, the room was carpeted with patterned wallpaper.

Patient 2.5.7 was brought into the room by one of the nurses and was seated in one of the arm chairs. Richard remained seated behind the desk and advised the nurse to take the rope with her. The patient looked weaker than the last time he had seen her and questioned the nurse. She explained that the patient had a meeting with Doctor De Ville earlier as it was a Wednesday and she wasn't used to being out of her room after that. Richard acknowledged her response and she left them alone.

It took a while to manage a conversation with 2.5.7.

"How are you feeling?" Richard asked.

She did not reply.

"Listen, 2.5.7," he said resting his elbows on the desk. "I hate calling you that. But I want to help you. And I need you to talk to me." She looked up at him weakly. "Do you remember the last time we met?"

She nodded.

"Who is the little girl?" His voice grew shaky.

"My friend Laurel," she replied. "She is the nicest one who comes to me."

"Comes to you? Why was she wet?"

"She," Patient 2.5.7 looked down with shame. "She died that way."

Richard was silent. He struggled to find words.

"She came to me my first day here to tell me that everything was going to be ok."

"The others," Richard began. He felt that was more important than the old man. "Do they have names?"

"Yes," she replied softly. "But I don't always know their names."

"Who are they?" He was thinking about Miss Brookes.

"When I was younger I called them monsters."

"Monsters? And now?"

"Some of them are still monsters. The shadowed ones are the scariest. But some; some I've learned are just lost."

"So you think they are real?"

"Well they used to be." Richard pulled a disconcerting expression.

"Because you think they died?"

"I knew you wouldn't believe me." Patient 2.5.7 lowered her head, and held herself tight. "You are not the one."

"I didn't say that." Richard felt the urge to hold her in his arms, but he resisted. He moved nearer however, to try and become more personal.

"Do you?"

"I come from a world of fact, believing in what I see. It is hard to grasp if I am honest."

"Then maybe you should open your eyes." The Patient looked so small in the large arm chair she was sitting in.

She sat up in her seat with a little more confidence in her tone. Richard saw it as a step. The patient was reaching out to him. He wanted to hold her; just for a moment. He wanted to show her he cared.

"I spoke with a nurse who used to look after you-"

"I know."

"You do?" he shifted in his seat.

"She's dying."

"You mean Nurse Enid Brookes? How do you know that?"

"She visits me." Richard tilted his head and wrote some notes on some paper. "She sometimes thinks she still works here and I have to tell her that she doesn't. When she realises that, she gets sad and goes away. Sometimes I avoid telling her so she stays a little longer, but something always reminds her that it's not the same as it used to be."

"Like what?"

"A different equipment used, or something not in its usual place. You see darkness fall within her eyes and her mouth drops. When she turns to me, I see her realisation and that's when she goes; sometimes with a tear in her eye. She regrets what she did. I know that. It doesn't stop it happening though."

Richard felt the emotion behind 2.5.7's voice. He had been leaning against the edge of the desk but stood up and came closer to her as she was speaking. He noticed her quiver as he approached. Her discoloured eyes sparkled in the dull lighting of his room. It had become dark outside while they were talking. It always seemed to get dark quickly.

"Can I ask you something?"

"You are my doctor." Richard smiled lightly and leaned against his desk.

"When I spoke to Nurse Brookes, she couldn't remember your name. Do you remember?"

"No, is it in my file?" she sounded hopeful.

"No I'm afraid not," Richard went to the file and flicked through it. "But I will find out."

"That is not all my file though." 2.5.7 pointed at the file Richard was holding. "The rest stays in my work room."

"Your work room?" Richard was confused. "Do you mean your bedroom?"

She did not reply but looked to her feet quietly.

"Is it in the basement?"

"How did you know? I am not supposed to talk about it." She moved forward in the chair.

"Doctor De Ville took you there today didn't he?" he knelt down beside her and hovered his hand over hers, which was gripping the arm of the chair tightly. He wanted to show her that he cared for her, but his thoughts were haunted by the voices of the others. He shouldn't touch her, especially when he thought about his visions last time.

He came so close that he felt the hairs on the back of her hand tickle his palm. He noticed she had new wounds on her arms. "I wish I knew your name," he whispered gently. "What does he do to you? Does he hurt you?"

All of a sudden, Patient 2.5.7 began to tremble. "They don't like you talking to me now."

"I don't care about them. I only care about you."

The lights flickered. Patient 2.5.7 moved away from Richard.

"Ignore them! Please ignore them!" Richard grabbed her by the upper arms tightly and as the lights continued to flicker, a dark figure formed behind the arm chair the patient was sat in. Richard's grip loosened as the figure shaped into a human form with blackened hair draping over the face. Patient 2.5.7 clung onto Richard and hid her face within his chest with his heart pounding vigorously.

The figure growled and leaned closer to them. Richard saw the grotesquely pointed teeth and the devil-like eyes as it breathed on him. "Get out!" it shouted in a loud low voice. But Richard did not budge he wrapped his arms around his patient and she rubbed her forehead against his chin.

"Tell it to go 2.5.7. You can control it."

The figure laughed when Richard spoke; and then he realised. The dark figure was the old patient that lived in room 2.5.7.

"Leave us!" Richard shouted.

As the figure expanded it rushed quickly towards them and Richard closed his eyes tightly as he felt the breeze of the figure run through both himself and Patient 2.5.7. They held each other tightly and within a moment the figure had gone and the lights had returned.

Suddenly Nurse Caddy came into the room to find Richard and the patient in an embrace. "What's going on?" she asked suspiciously with an attitude. Patient

2.5.7 pulled away from Richard and cowered in the corner. Richard did not respond. “Well?”

“We were talking,” Richard did not know what else to say. He turned to Patient 2.5.7 and offered his hand to help her to her feet but she did not take it. She stood up by herself. Nurse Caddy was holding the rope she was to be tied to. “I better take you to your room.” She offered the rope. “You’ve had a too busy day today.”

“I’m sorry,” Richard said. He felt an unwarranted amount of guilt; like he had been caught with another lover or something. Of course he didn’t feel that way for his patient. But he did not understand what he was feeling. Nurse Caddy took the patient to her room and was to meet with Richard back at their shared room in the Nurses House. It became clear to Richard that she was worried about the connection forming between himself and Patient 2.5.7. She had seen what had happened to others who had crossed the path with Patient 2.5.7. But Richard was sure this was different.

V

Richard climbed into his bed within Nurse Caddy’s room. He was wearing his striped pyjamas. Chloe had not spoken while she got ready for bed. In her skimpy nighty, she also climbed into her own bed this time and fluffed her pillows up.

“Are we alright Chloe?” Richard asked with a certain amount of hesitancy in his voice. The essence of awkwardness aired within the room like a toxic gas.

She turned to him with raised eyebrows as she began removing her makeup from her face. “Well I don’t know Rick? Are we?” She turned back to her mirror.

Richard was unsure how to tackle the question. There was an awkward pause before he answered. “I want to be.”

“What were you doing with the patient?” Chloe queried bluntly.

“If I am honest, I don’t know.” Chloe huffed angrily as he answered. “But I think I believe her.”

“You believe her how?” she swivelled her body to face him with only the gap between the beds keeping them apart.

“She sees things Chlo. And she showed me.” Richard was passionate about his feelings and Chloe could see it. She was jealous. “If only I knew what brought her to the asylum in the first place.”

Chloe bit her bottom lip and lowered her head to avert her eyes from his. He pressed her for an explanation and she explained that she knew how Patient 2.5.7 had come to the asylum in the first place.

"She was found with a dead body in the woods near her house," she described the scene like she had been there. Chloe's eyes filled with tears as she spoke. The description of a little defenceless girl standing in a pool of muddy blood, over a body of a man who had been stabbed multiple times, was not the easiest things to explain.

"But she was a child? How could she have done anything like that?" Richard did not comprehend the logic in a little girl killing a grown man.

"I do not know but her parents were the ones who felt it best to protect her and themselves by her being in here." Chloe was still hiding something; Richard could tell.

"They should be in her file."

"They are." Chloe held herself tight.

"What?!" Richard took her hands in his, still with the gap between them of the separation of the beds. He wanted an explanation.

"I wasn't sure whether I should give this to you, but;" Chloe reached for her bag on the chair near her bed. She scrambled through it for a moment until revealing a tidily folded piece of paper. She passed it to him and joined him on his bed.

When Richard unfolded it, the paper was very delicate. It disclosed the contact information for the parents. Their names; their address; their telephone number.

"Miss Eleanor Walton," Richard stated, almost choking on his words. He didn't understand his emotions. "She has a name." With excitement, he kissed Chloe hard on the cheek. She smiled and got under the covers ready to go to sleep.

It took a little longer for Richard to settle for the night. He stared at the first page of Patient 2.5.7's file. He decided he was to visit the parents. He needed to. He needed to understand what happened with the 6 year old Miss Eleanor Walton, to make her become Patient 2.5.7 that was now twenty seven years old. Her mystical knowledge of people frightened him and captivated his senses so much so that any information to help him explain her would ease his thoughts.

Chapter Seven: Richard Meets the Parents

Richard looked carefully in the mirror as he did his tie. His hands were shaking. He had been standing there for a good ten minutes before Chloe came over to help him with it. After straightening the tie she brushed his shoulders with her hands and kissed him on the cheek. She wanted to go with Richard but he felt it was best that he went alone, even though he was nervous. He borrowed her old banger of a car, which chugged along the road like it could break down any moment. The exhaust fumes followed him for a few miles. He imagined people choking on it still a few days later.

At certain points of his journey he stopped to check the map before often turning around to try different route. This meant driving through the smog he had already created with the exhaust fumes. He almost started choking himself. It ended being a longer drive than he expected, what with the wrong turns. It was early afternoon.

The street seemed presentable and he parked by the pavement, where the car gave one loud bang to confirm it had come to a stop. Richard took a deep breath before he began to walk down the street. He straightened his tie.

In the row of terraces he passed he counted the numbers, until he reached the house he believed must be the one. He had seen the house before. It was in a number of Patient 2.5.7's drawings, especially the obvious early ones. There was a small garden in front with little grass and a little rusted black painted gate for an entrance.

First, Richard checked the address before stepping any further. He didn't want to knock the wrong one. Having the folded piece of paper in his jacket pocket, he pulled it out to check and then stuffed it back in like he was trying to hide something rude.

The gate squeaked as he opened it and the ground was a little crumbly as he tread. He knocked little to begin with. Then he gave an official knock to the door. He felt he was going to sell something with the type of knock he gave. There was no answer. He wasn't sure what to do now. He had come all that way, which wasn't very far but felt like it with his geographically skills.

"They won' be in yet," an old woman commented, popping her head out of her front window next door. "She goes shopping on Wednesday afternoons."

"Do you know what time they will be back?" Richard replied politely. The window was slammed and in a few moments, the neighbour's front door opened. "An hour or so? What do you want them for?" she stood in her dress and slippers, shivering slightly with the cold breeze that had just set in.

"Oh just some help with something." He moved away and decided to have a walk round the neighbourhood while he waited.

"You're not selling something then?" the elderly woman questioned and Richard nodded, now out of the boundaries of Patient 2.5.7's childhood home. "I didn't think so. The other men like you didn't sell anything either." The old woman started walking back into her own house.

"Other men like me? What do you mean?" he moved closer to her front gate. He was unsure whether he was just being paranoid.

"Oh it was years ago now!" she waved her duster in the air. "But you all look the same you doctors. The same judgemental stare, like you've got a horrible smell under your nose."

Richard looked down at his appearance. "How? How did you know I was a doctor?"

"I'm an old woman son! I've seen plenty of doctors in my time." She leaned against her door post until she jumped up like an angry cat and spoke quickly. "Not ones like you though. I'm not nuts!" She waved her duster in the air again.

"So doctors like me; did they come here often?"

"Only when the girl was there. What was her name? She's probably dead now god rest her soul." She paused and tapped her chin with thought.

"Eleanor?"

"No, no wasn't that." She spoke still considering the options. "I know. It was Nelly. Never saw that girl again; the last time one of you came here, they took her away."

"Nelly?" Richard smiled picturing Patient 2.5.7 as Nelly. She suited it; more so than Eleanor. He leaned on the old woman's gate with both his hands.

"Strangest thing when they took her away." She paused and thought again for moment. "Your questions are about her again aren't they?"

"Yes, they are."

She went inside and left her front door open as a gesture for him to follow. When he did, the hallway was quite dark but with flowery walls in every room. He joined her in the living room. "Now," she began as she sat down on her chair. "This girl was strange and nuts don't get me wrong, but she was so cute. I remember when she was born; her parents were so in love. But then she grew up a little."

"What happened as she grew up a little?" Richard shifted in the sofa. It was claustrophobically soft.

"I was friend with Nelly's Grandfather. He was a lovely man; such a gentleman. And he was the only one who would allow that little girl to have an imagination. Then he passed away God rest his soul."

"How did that effect Patient – I mean Nelly?"

"Well it didn't that's the strange part."

"She still spoke to him and laughed with him."

"Do you know why?" Richard was hesitant when asking. He didn't want this to sound like a consultation.

"Well 'cause she was mental of course," the old woman replied with an obvious sort of tone.

"How did you come to that conclusion?"

"It's a little obvious when the child talked to herself the majority of the time."

"All children have a tendency to have an imaginary friend."

"Not like this they didn't. My kids had one at some point but it was the 'friends' that she had." The old woman rocked in her seat.

"Can you expand?"

"Sometimes when she described who she saw, they were strange people, sometimes gruesome people. The child had too much imagination and that wasn't right."

"So the doctors who came?"

"Oh there was only one doctor that came to visit. Can't remember his name now?" she pondered a moment.

"Was it Doctor De Ville?"

"That could be it. It was foreign anyway."

"And he came often?"

"Oh yes. And the last time I saw him was the last time I saw that little insane girl. She was crying! Oh the tears! The whole street was out staring!"

Richard's heart hurt as he listened to the gruesome story. The whispers; the judgment; the fear. He felt sickened by the thought that his patient was terrified by the adults that surrounded her.

Suddenly there was a squeak of a gate. Someone was home next door. "That'll be her home now; Mrs Walton." The elderly woman showed him to the door with the creaking of her old bones. He thanked the old lady for the information that she had given him and went straight to the front door, knocking in a professional manner. This time a late middle aged lady answered. Her hair was a dyed brown that she had been trying to keep natural. She was turning grey.

"Yes?" she asked.

"Hi, my name is Doctor Richard Pearce. Are you Mrs Walton?"

"Yes?" Her eyes shivered with concern.

"I work for Gravehill Asylum-"

"No thank you." She tried to shut the door but Richard placed his foot in the way.

"Please Mrs Walton, I won't take up too much of your time. I only have a few questions is all. I want to help your daughter."

"I don't have a daughter."

"Please?"

"NO!" she slammed the door onto his foot and he pulled away with pain. He hopped to the gate and sighed disappointed in her reaction. He turned back at the house and saw Mrs Walton peeking through the curtains of the front window. He looked at his watch. If he left now, he would make it in time for dinner with Chloe.

Walking back to his car, he took one last look at the terrace house and pulled out a picture from his inside pocket. He leaned on the car and stared at the photograph. It was of the patient. The one he had taken of her in one of his earlier consultations. He saw the sadness in her eyes. He felt he had failed her.

"Is that her now?" a voice asked from behind him. He turned and it was Mrs Walton. "I'm sorry I hurt your foot." He smiled dimly and gave her the photo. "She looks exactly the same as when I left her." Richard stood up straight from leaning on the bonnet of the car. "Why are you asking questions now?"

"Because I want to know her Mrs Walton," he replied placing the picture back in his inner pocket. "I believe her."

"You believe her?" She turned and walked back to the house. "You can't stay too long mind, my husband is due back soon and if he knew you were here!"

"That's fine." Richard spoke with a calming and reassuring tone.

She brought out a pot of tea and they sat at the dining table quietly. Eventually, Mrs Walton asked Richard what he wanted to know and he explained that he wanted answers as to why Patient 2.5.7 was admitted to Gravehill Asylum.

She explained that the stories she would say about people they knew or even people they didn't were frightening and it became clear the teachers in school did not want her in class because of it. It scared the other children. She struggled to make friends that were real because of it too and then Doctor De Ville came out of nowhere for a random visit.

"So you didn't ask for a consultation with him?"

"He telephoned asking to meet her," her voice was shaky as she spoke and the cup and saucer jingled against one another as she gripped them tightly. "He asked to meet her and Mr Walton; my husband; he thought it was best for all of us. Especially after my father passed."

Richard remembered what the next door neighbour had said about him. "I see," he responded. "So after he took her away, why have you not visited her?"

"Doctor De Ville felt it was best and my husband agreed." She sounded disappointed with the decision, even after all this time. "There was something else as well," she began. "You may have noticed yourself when speaking with her."

"What's that?"

"The things she knew that has never been spoken. Secrets; truths; nightmares. She knew things a child shouldn't even dream about. She wasn't normal doctor."

"And when that man died in the woods? What happened then?"

"We found her soaked in blood by the man's dead body in the woods. She didn't say anything she just stuttered and mumbled things we couldn't comprehend. We called Doctor De Ville straight away and he took her straight to the asylum. The police were obviously involved but De

Ville protected her. He said she would remain under his care."

"Was it proven that she did anything?"

"Never, but it is the only logical explanation that she had done something. She had mentioned something about it earlier in the week about someone dying in the woods. But I never wanted to believe it."

"If you could only see her again, you wouldn't believe she could do such a thing." Richard leaned forward putting his arms on the table.

"If that's the case it's because Doctor De Ville is curing her."

"Do you think you could visit her soon? I know she'd love it."

"No. I couldn't. My husband would... No."

"Please Mrs Walton. I believe you could be good for her. She needs contact." He took Mrs Walton's hand in his.

"No. You really need to go now." She stood up and removed herself from the enticement. "My husband will be home soon."

"Please Mrs Walton. Here me out."

Suddenly a car pulled up outside. "He's home!" Mrs Walton gasped and tried to hurry Richard out, but it was too late. Mr Walton stared at him as he entered his home.

“Who’s this?” he asked gruffly. He was a slightly overweight man around fifty five. His hair was dark and his face was scruffy.

“My name is Doctor Richard Pearce.” Richard said firmly and held out his hand for a greeting. “I work at the asylum where your daughter currently resides at.”

“What?” he growled. “What are you doing in my house?”

“Honey! He had a few questions so I didn’t see the harm-”

“NO!” he yelled and grabbed Richard by the scruff of the neck, shoving him against the wall. “We put this behind us when we left that thing in that place. Get out!”

“Ok!” Richard croaked and held up his hands. “Ok!” Mr Walton shoved him out the door, where he fell to the ground. “She just needs someone to care about her. That’s all!”

Mr Walton ran at Richard and punched him in the face, screaming at him to leave. Richard went to the car and still holding his hand over his eye, he drove off quickly. His head was throbbing. He needed to see his patient.

Chapter Eight: October 1956 – Richard Finally Cracks

The sunlight had almost gone by the time Richard got back to the asylum. He parked the car within the grounds and rushed across the gravel into the building. Reaching the reception, he slowed his pace so not to cause any abnormalities. He greeted the nurse behind the desk and continued through to the stairs. He walked slowly, taking each step as a breath. Reaching the second floor he greeted the nurse at the table. He requested to see Patient 2.5.7.

"I'm afraid you can't," the nurse stated hardly looking up at him. When he questioned her, she made the passing comment that Doctor De Ville had already taken her for a consultation.

"It's not Wednesday!" Richard snapped at the nurse, spitting a little.

"Listen Doctor, Nurse Caddy came to me and said she needed the key for Patient 2.5.7's room as Doctor De Ville needs to see his patient urgently. I do not know anything else."

"Nurse Caddy is not working this evening though?"

"Well she was when she came here to me."

Richard growled and stormed away from the table. He ran up the stairs to the top floor, skipping over a step at a time. Racing down the corridor his barged into Doctor De Ville's room without knocking.

The room was empty.

Richard groaned angrily and hit his fist on De Ville's desk with frustration. The room was quite dark as the light had dimmed outside and the curtains were open a mere inch. Richard took a few deep breaths to gather his thoughts. He stared blindly at the books on the shelves. They were dusty and untouched. But one was not. Richard pulled it from its place and studied the cover. It was experimentation. Surgical techniques. More importantly brain surgery. In the same location as the book, he found old photographs of patients, before and after. The patients, Richard did not recognise. They all had scars across their heads in the 'after' photographs.

He moved quickly, leaving the book open on a page with an image of a brain being cut open. The photos were also left. As he ran down the stairs, he tripped skidded down one of the flights. He took a few seconds to recover and as he clambered onto all fours he noticed two feet in front of him. It was Matron.

Richard groaned again; partly due to his pain in his back after falling down about twenty stairs. "Come with me. Say nothing," she said sternly. She swivelled around and continued down the corridor. She didn't help him to his feet, so he pushed himself up and caught up to her. They came to the end of the corridor and reached the lift within the wall. Matron revealed a very old rusted key from her pocket. She pulled the chain on lift gate and unlocked the padlock. Once the chain was removed, she stepped aside for Richard to assist her in opening the gate.

It's screeched open slowly and when Richard glanced at Matron, she had a grave expression on her face. "Be careful when you go down there. I didn't take you here."

Richard nodded and stepped inside the lift carefully. The gate was shut from the outside and he descended in the dimmed lighted lift down to the basement.

The lift chugged like a dying car and screeched to a halt. He forced the door open and he came to a wall. The lighting was still dim and Richard walked from one end of the passage to the other. There was no door.

The space was becoming airless and Richard began to feel like the walls were closing in. He rubbed his hands against the wall, searching for an opening. Then something clicked. One brick was pushed in further and created a crack run down the wall. He managed to push an opening from the crack to walk through.

He entered a room that was cobwebbed and had a row of old empty beds inside. As Richard walked through the room, he saw the stained mattresses that looked like a mixture of old blood, urine and sick on it.

Richard heard a man's voice in the distance so he followed through to the next room. The doors were the traditional two-way, so he pushed it lightly so not to create too much noise. It was a thin passageway. The doors that followed were all open except the one on the end. It was Doctor De Ville's voice that Richard could hear, which was coming from that room. He widened his steps and hurried to the door.

"Now Patient 2.5.7, this is going to sting at first," Richard heard Doctor De Ville say.

"I'm sorry," Patient 2.5.7 sobbed.

Richard rushed into the room! The patient was laying on the surgical table with wires connected to her temples. She was clamped to the table by wooden braces and Doctor De Ville was perched at a machine with his hand on the lever.

"Pearce!" De Ville gasped. "You are just in time to assist me in making our patient better." He had a wild look in his eyes that Richard had never seen before. "That is a lovely black eye forming there I see?" He turned to his patient and she had tears in her eyes with a wooden mouth piece keeping her mouth open.

"What are you doing to her?" Richard took her hand that was restricted at the wrist by the clamp.

"It's your fault you know."

"How?"

"You had to pick her. Didn't you? She is mine. She is the only one I have control over. The others? There are rules now. You cannot cure these people and now we can't even try. This is my last patient I can try."

"By electrocuting them?! This is madness!"

"This ward used to be-"

"This ward is torture! You hurt patients to shut them up." Richard tugged at one of the clamps. "I've seen the photos De Ville."

"Stand back Pearce!" De Ville shoved him from the table and pulled the lever. Patient 2.5.7 began to fit by the electrical volts pulsing through her body.

"Stop!" Richard growled. He hit De Ville with a nearby surgical hammer and turned the machine off.

Patient 2.5.7 sighed with relief. With De Ville on the floor, Richard stroked her forehead and removed the wood piece from her mouth. "It's alright Nelly," he whispered. "I'm here."

A tear ran down her cheek, she couldn't bring herself to say anything to him. She lifted her hand from her wrist and tugged at the bottom of his jacket as that was all she could reach still being clamped down. Richard smiled down at her and gently leaned over and kissed her on her forehead.

He felt her yearn for him as he kissed her, feeling her want to kiss him back. He was transported to her memories; she was letting him see. She was a lot younger and there were other patients there. He saw the row of beds that he had seen before but with patients laying in them. Doctor De Ville was there, also looking younger, utilising the instruments that Richard has seen in the other room.

De Ville took each patient in a room and electrocuted them while asking them questioned. There was an evil smile on De Ville's face as he revelled in the pain it was causing them. He felt the pain and loneliness of his patient, until she showed him the day they first met.

When Richard lifted his head from kissing her, he returned back into the room. There was a knowing gaze between them but as he looked into Nelly's eyes, he saw her expression change to fear.

He took too long to turn around! Doctor De Ville wacked Richard on the side of his head. He pulled the lever again and the volts shot through Nelly as well as Richard. He felt his nerves vibrate uncontrollably and the shooting pain caused his heart to triple in speed. Richard saw flashes of light.

He felt himself crumble to the floor onto his knees. He started to see flickering images of the past events. Nelly was a little girl. She was standing at the entrance of the woods. All of a sudden a man was standing next to her. She only noticed him after something dripped on her. It was his blood, dripping from his chest. The man had paled and his chest had been sliced numerous times. Richard felt Nelly's nervousness, but she followed the man into the woods.

The ground was uneven and Nelly tripped a couple of times. She lost a shoe at one point and as she tried to retrieve it, the man growled at her appearing very close to her face so she continued taking off her other shoe to make it easier to run.

Finally she came to a clearing. And found the man's body on the floor. She squelched through the mud to stand by him and then looked up at the man's ghost who was still with her. He pointed in the direction of a shadowed part of the woods. She saw a man hovering behind a tree and when he revealed himself Richard was stunned in seeing the man was Doctor De Ville. He lifted his finger in front of his lips and hushed the little six year old Nelly.

"Never say a word little girl and you will never be harmed," he whispered to her. He had a knife in his hand.

Suddenly there were noises of people coming closer and De Ville rushed away throwing the knife at Nelly's feet. She inadvertently picked it up and held it in her palm.

As the image faded from Richard's vision he saw the police arriving.

Richard felt the pain of electrocution ease and he panted heavily, staring at the green tiled flooring he had knelt on. "It was you," he hissed.

"What?" De Ville sensed an unnerving truth surfacing.

"You killed that man and it was you who blamed the child." Richard carefully stood up, feeling woozy.

"I don't know what you-"

"Yes!" Richard shouted. "Yes you do. Who was that man? And why blame it on an innocent child?" He ached everywhere.

"He was a former doctor here who disagreed with our methods here. He was going to tell the authorities and when I made him a patient, he escaped. It was the only way!"

"And why Nelly? Why her?" Richard gestured to Patient 2.5.7 laying on the table breathing deeply.

"She was saying things. She was saying things about patients in here that she shouldn't know about. She needed to be stopped. And the best way to do that was to keep her locked away in here." De Ville picked up a scalpel that was on the side. Richard stood in front of Nelly to protect her.

"So you do this to her to keep her quiet?"

"I did it to all my patients and she learnt her lessons well until you came along." He pointed the scalpel at him aggressively. "Now Pearce. I am afraid you know too much. So you will not be able to work here anymore."

"I would never want to work here again after seeing this!"

"Good. But I am afraid I cannot let you leave either." A darkened grin appeared on De Ville's face as he moved closer to Richard, who had nothing to grasp in defence.

He took Nelly's hand as he felt behind him. He squeezed tightly.

De Ville lifted the scalpel and unexpectedly stabbed his own arm. He screamed with the pain and just as Richard's mouth dropped with alarm, De Ville grabbed him and stabbed him, not with the scalpel but with a needle.

Richard's legs were the first to go. Everything was beginning to feel numb. And just before everything went black, he heard the distancing laughter of De Ville. He had won.

Chapter Nine: Intensive Ward

The sound of humming wakened Richard from his sleep. He yawned uncontrollably and as he moved, he felt the clanking on chains against his wrists and ankles. He opened his eyes to see his bare feet merely brushing the floor with his toes. His head was heavy, but as he lifted himself to become accustomed to his surroundings, he realised he was in a padded cell, like the one he had seen in the intensive ward.

The humming was coming from the adjacent cell and echoed through the emptiness of the ward. Richard's mouth was dry. He coughed a couple of times. He heard the door that was in front of him unlock. It was pulled open and Nurse Caddy appeared with a glass of water.

"Chloe," he breathed with relief.

"Shh," she hushed and offered her glass to his dry cracked lips.

Taking a few sips he held the water in his mouth for a moment before swallowing to savour it. "How long have-"

"Two weeks today Ricky," she said quietly. "I have been waiting for you to wake."

He smiled sentimentally, but then his thoughts gathered and he remembered the basement. He shook about trying to get free. “I need to get out of here. De Ville is a villain!”

“SHH!” Chloe put her hand on his chest to stop him from struggling. “It’s no use. Doctor De Ville has explained how you had become ill like many who have been in contact Patient 2.5.7.”

“You know that is not true Chlo? Surely?”

She lowered her head. “Listen, I have been working closely with Doctor De Ville these passed weeks. I think you need a rest; that is all.” She left him shouting after her; begging her to help him. He didn’t see the tears in her eyes has she went.

He shook the chains and screamed out for Patient 2.5.7, until finally he began sobbing to himself.

He heard the nurse, Pamela, in the next cell giggling. She had warned him that this word happen. Eventually he stopped trying to convince the nurses who came in to feed him that he was sane. He hung there silently. Left alone with his own thoughts riled him so that he began thinking he was seeing things that were not really there.

I mustn’t say anything. They must not know.

He chanted in his mind these words so not to show the madness that was forming within his loneliness.

Weeks had passed. It was turning into months. The number of weeks were left unknown to Richard. The door was unlocked and it was Matron who had entered this time. Richard thought it must be a mirage; he had not seen her since he was free, but when he saw her serious expression it worried him into hoping it was just a mirage.

She took hold of one of the locks on Richard legs and by unlocking that one, it released him to the floor. Richard wobbled with the feeling of holding his own weight. She unlocked the others so he was free. Feeling his sore wrists and legs from the chains, he was hesitant to say anything to her.

"You must go," she stated plainly.

"Matron, I-"

"Patient 2.5.7 needs you. Go to her. The operation is going to take place and I; well you're the one who can stop him."

Richard only heard the word operation and he was lost within his knowledge of what Doctor De Ville had been planning. He was going to operate of Nelly's brain to keep her quiet permanently. He ran clumsily down the corridor of the Intensive Ward and passed the nurse who was in charge of locking the metal barred gate. The floor felt like it just had been cleaned as he slipped a few times. On running passed the kitchen door, it was opened and he knocked the person over who was walking through it at the time. "Sorry!" Richard shouted as he continued to run.

Passing many nurses as he made his way to the lift, he ignored their mouths dropping in horror at the sight of him. None of them stopped him. None of them said anything. They just watched. The chain was already unlocked when he reached the lift. The screech echoed through the asylum's corridor that Richard thought sounded like the screams of the dead – the victims of De Ville's evil.

By the time he ran through the room with the row of disgusting rotten beds, he glimpsed a nurse's hat that appeared from the room he had found his patient previously.

"Rick!"

Richard faltered in his mission. He looked down at the face of the nurse. It was Chloe. It sickened him to think she of all people was helping De Ville with his actions. She spoke again. "Ricky, what are you doing here? How did you get out?"

He ignored her questions. "Where is she?" he muttered in a serious voice with no warmth in his tone.

"It's for the best Rick." Chloe tried to reason with him but he shoved her aside, entering the room.

As soon as Patient 2.5.7 saw him she wailed. "Doctor!" she yelled. Doctor De Ville had been preparing himself for surgery. He grabbed one of the knives on the side table, but Richard was ready this time!

He grabbed the old doctor's wrist and bashed it against the wall so hard that one of the green tiles cracked. De Ville dropped the knife and Richard head butted him hard. With De Ville falling to the floor with pain, Richard scrambled to Patient 2.5.7 and began to release her straps. "We're getting out of here Nelly," he said kindly as he rushed to free her. One arm had been made free and she instantly touched his face gently rubbing her thumb of his bottom lip that was cracked and sore.

"Thank you," she whispered. "Richard." He felt her yearning for him. He yearned for to hold her too.

One of her legs became free too.

Suddenly, De Ville screamed and ran at Richard with the same knife he had been holding and managed to scrape his arm. Richard hissed with the pain and they fought each other in a scuffle. He was strong for an older man.

Chloe had returned to the room and tried to stop them fighting. It wasn't working. She caught the eye of Patient 2.5.7 and she whispered to the nurse to release her other hand. Chloe hesitated but she believed in Richard so loosened the straps for the Patient to free herself.

“Richard!” she shouted. At that point there had been a break in the scuffle and both Richard and De Ville glanced at the patient. She freed her other leg and threw herself at De Ville, clutching his head tightly in both hands. They simultaneously felt a burning sensation and Richard swore he could see smoke. Both of them screaming in agony, De Ville pulled her off him and when he opened his eyes, he saw all the patients he had harmed and then killed over the years. All of them had become more and more hideous by their waiting to take there revenge on him. He ran into the larger room where the row of beds were, trying to hit things away from him that only he could see. The other three followed him. Chloe came to Richard attempting to ease his aches from fighting.

And then a smell came upon them like a ship in the night. It was smoke. It was coming from the above floors. “There’s a fire!” Chloe said, holding tight to Richard.

Suddenly, De Ville’s screams were even louder as instruments began to move on their own. Both Richard and Chloe watching in horror as the knives flew in De Ville’s direction. “Is that you?” Richard turned to Nelly, but she was just as horrified as they were.

She didn’t reply, but he knew it was her. She didn’t take her eyes of him!

De Ville begged for help but the place was beginning to get warmer and the smoke was making it harder to see.

Eventually, the knives fell to the floor because the smoke had become too thick. Richard grabbed a hand of each woman and tugged them to the lift. Chloe pulled him and in doing so, pulled the patient down the thin corridor that seemed like a dead end to Richard, but she revealed a flight of old crumbly stairs.

As they made their way up there Chloe fell and twisted her ankle. Richard picked her up in his arms while trying to keep hold of Nelly, but Nelly let go. "You can't hold both of us," she explained. "I am right behind you." He carried Chloe up the steps, avoiding the certain steps that looked more crumbly. Reaching a door, Chloe opened it and they rushed through, where they were met with the fire. It had spread all the way through the asylum.

Richard didn't stop to think about where he was, he looked out for natural light and as soon as he saw a window he smashed through it and ran outside seeing all the nurses, doctors and patients already outside. Richard fell to his knees and placed Chloe down onto the ground where they were met by paramedics. "A twisted ankle and severe smoke intoxication," Richard stated. "And-" He turned to Nelly, but she wasn't there. "Where is she?" he stood up quickly and looked around him. "Where has she gone?"

“I didn’t see her come out with us,” Chloe said, while been assisted by one of the paramedics.

Richard’s heart pounded and the other paramedic who had come to help them tried to calm him down. “I need to go back him!” he moved towards the building.

“No Sir,” the paramedic said, but Richard continued. The firemen had just arrived and Richard pulled away from them as they attempted to stop him.

He punched one of them as they gripped his arm tightly and he ran inside the fiery building. The smoke was thicker that before. He screamed out her name but there was no response. He moved slowly through the smog and got more and more lost. Then he saw something. It was a little girl. She stood, still sopping wet like he had seen her before. It was Laurel. She pointed in one direction and he followed her gesture. Then she appeared again; showing him the way. He recognised his location he had come to the crumbling stairs.

He moved swiftly down them and called for her again. He heard his name and with excitement he moved faster. Finally he found her... the ceiling had caved in and created a barrier that she was unable to climb over.

“Nelly, are you alright?” Richard called.

“Yes Richard. I’m scared.”

"Don't be. I'm here." He pulled at the debris, trying to clear some of it and made a hole just big enough for her to crawl through. He took her hand from the other side and she struggled through. And once she managed to jump down he held her tightly in his arms, kissing her on the top of her head for a long moment. He kissed her again on her nose. He had thought he had lost her. He felt her crying and he hushed her reassuring her everything was going to be alright.

They moved upwards and this time Richard did not let go of her hand. They made out of the basement and just as they passed the lift Richard heard Nelly scream and he lost her hand. He turned back and she had fallen to the floor but De Ville gripping her ankle from the grid of the gate. Richard kicked his hand away from her and pulled her away from him.

"You will die with me," De Ville growled and when Richard turned to where the escape was, it had been blocked by the fire. De Ville was scared and bleeding from the attack in the basement.

"GO!" screamed a woman's voice suddenly. It was Matron. "Take her and go." Richard lifted Nelly into his arms and she held him tightly. Matron held something with her apron pocket that she did not reveal to him. "Save her. I have Doctor De Ville."

Richard nodded and ran through the fire, making their escape. He heard a distant bang as he met the firemen just at the reception and rushed out. He fell to the ground, landing on his bum, still clutching Nelly in his arms. As the paramedics came to assist, he told them to leave them be. He didn't want to let her go.

"I'm a doctor. I will check she is alright!" he snapped and they kept their distance. It took both Richard and Nelly an age to release each other from their hold. Nelly looked at the building that was still on fire. Each window smoking and burning.

"They are smiling," she said with relief like a weight had been lifted.

"The patients?"

"They can move one now. They are free."

"And so are you Nelly." Richard was still hovering his arms around her and as he spoke she turned to look at him. "You are free too." She hugged him tightly and he held her again. "Thank the little girl before she goes for you."

Nelly looked up at him confused.

"She showed me to you. I wanted her to be thanked before she moved on."

"She's not."

"Why?"

"She isn't finished with this world yet. She wasn't a patient." Richard was about to question her but Chloe limped towards them. She tugged at Richard to stand and when he did she kissed him passionately on the lips.

Nelly looked back at the asylum that she had been locked away inside for so many years. The building was dying and the dead that scared her, didn't seem scary anymore. She watched their lights fly to the sky. She felt their peace.

They were free.

She was free.

PART TWO:

TIMES ARE CHANGING

Chapter Nine: 2014 An Old Doctor's Story

"That's a real intense story Robert," Joe said as he stretched.

"That poor patient?" Kirsty breathed. "It shows how medicine has changed I suppose."

"It's not that," Richard explained in his old creaky voice. "It just shows there are evil people in the world." He looked at Kirsty and then at Joe. It was getting quite late and both their shifts would be ending soon. He gazed out the window, while he gathered his thoughts.

"Did you marry Chloe?" Kirsty asked. "Ooo and what happened to Patient 2.5.7?"

"I think those questions can be answered another time," Joe said getting up from the bed. "It's getting late and Richard needs his rest.

Kirsty sighed and followed him out. "I'll be back tomorrow Richard! Don't you worry!" She saw Richard roll his eyes as they closed the door behind them.

As they walked through the carpeted corridor to the stairs, Joe looked back at the door like he was considering something. Kirsty also stopped to wait for him and stared at him for an answer.

"It's a convincing story isn't it," Joe said continuing down the stairs, with his hands in his pockets.

"What do you mean? Don't you believe him?"

"Well no. Everyone knows that the 'famous Doctor Pearce' is a fabric of his imagination. He was a patient in that Gravehill place." Joe opened the door and let Kirsty walk through first.

"You're serious?"

"Yeah." He shrugged his shoulders and they reached the open air.

"Wow." Kirsty found it hard to believe because it was so detailed.

"If I were you I wouldn't bother him with the story again." Joe was walking away as he spoke. "You probably have someone else to see tomorrow anyway."

"He doesn't seem to like visitors," she joked as she began walking in the opposite direction.

"Exactly!"

Richard had been watching them from the window. He took a long deep breath as he opened his palm to find that photograph of his wife. A tear fell as he gazed at it. He got to his feet slowly and walked with his old creaky bones to his wardrobe. Looking inside he found his old scarf. It seemed quite tattered with dodgy stitching in places. He rubbed his thumb over his stitched letters that spelt out his name and put it on.

He rummaged around inside the wardrobe again and found one of his old psychology books. He brought it to his desk and let it fall open, finding an old cloth inside. He lifted it carefully like it could disintegrate at any moment. He unfolded it and old faded numbers were on it. Those numbers were 2.5.7. He smiled fondly.

Chapter Ten: 1957 – Building A Life

It was a good few months before Richard and Chloe were fully settled in their new flat they had begun to rent together. They were situated opposite each other, but they generally shared one of the flats. This time as an official couple. Chloe had done the decorating and although both flats were small, they were cosy. They shared the main bedroom in one flat, while Nelly was given the spare one. Richard had refused to allow Nelly to be taken to another asylum ignoring Chloe's concerns about her safety. He also disagreed with Chloe's idea for Nelly to stay in the other flat on her own.

Nelly spent her days locked in the apartment, while both Chloe and Richard worked full time. Richard had found it quite difficult to find another job. He had returned to his university to assist his old professor in lecturing, while he looked for a permanent position as a doctor. Chloe had found a new job quite quickly and continued to work with many of the other nurses who had lost their jobs after the closure of Gravehill Asylum.

Eventually, Richard found a place working in a hospital, specialising in psychiatrics. Although it had hard hours, Richard always rushed home to spend time with Nelly before Chloe came home. They would spend the hour talking about Nelly's night terrors and the people she could see. Chloe did not like Richard talking to her with so much interest. And Richard's relentless intent to take Nelly outside, worried Chloe as she felt the patient could be aggressive to someone or 'take a turn' and it would be she and Richard who would be in trouble for not putting her away.

Without the medication, she was given whilst growing up, Nelly was gaining her own identity; being able to decide whether she liked or disliked something, although Chloe would often correct her if she disagreed. "Yes Nurse Caddy," was often repeated within the tiny apartment. Nelly was still beginning to become more confident in her own understandings and decisions however. Chloe had increasing concern over this as weeks turned into months she saw Richard and the *patient* become closer in her absence during work times. She continued to treat Nelly like a patient and a child, refusing to let her ask questions. But as Chloe's jealousy became more intense, she realised she had to do something to stop Richard from losing his self-control.

Although it was several months and Nelly had made certain progress, her screams in the night and her supposed self-harming had not improved from being away from Gravehill. And on a certain night, it was the last straw.

Chloe had planned a romantic evening. She had locked Nelly within her room, while she prepared a dinner for two. During the night, Chloe enticed Richard into their bedroom with a new sexy nightie. They started kissing while in bed together, but Richard heard a whimper in the spare room. He looking in the direction of the door.

When he turned back to Chloe, he heard something again. “I need to check on her,” he said, leaving Chloe frustrated. As he left his bedroom, he heard the click of the light that Chloe had turned off. He was not welcome to return.

He found Nelly crying quietly in her room, so he joined her on the bed. “What is it?” he asked, wanting to hold her in his arms.

“Nothing,” she croaked.

“Go on,” he nudged her playfully.

“I keep seeing the green floor and the walls. And.” She stopped talking and climbed out of the bed. Richard looked at the space on the bed where Nelly had been positioned and a wet patch remained. She had wet herself.

“That doesn’t matter,” he said pulling the sheet off the bed. “Why don’t we sleep on the floor tonight?” he laid blankets and pillows on the floor and the slept all night. Chloe found them together and realised something needed to be done to rid the third person in the relationship.

On a day that was quite dismal to say the least, Chloe had booked a half day at her work and met Richard at his. She, knowing he would be able to leave anytime, surprised him with a romantic night away. Richard did not seem fussed at first but by seeing the disappointment in his girlfriend's eyes, he agreed. Chloe had explained she had called Nelly an hour earlier to let her know and made her food ready so she would not have to use anything in the kitchen.

She had lied.

Earlier that day, Chloe had given Nelly the same drug she had taken for years during her time in Gravehill, knowing that it caused her 'hallucinations' to spiral out of control, since she had not taken it in almost a year.

"Now, 2.5.7," Chloe said as crushed the drug into a glass of water. "Ricky is coming home early today and wants to take you out."

"Ok Nurse Caddy." Nelly glugged the drink down excitedly.

"But you need to sit and wait for him to return. Alright?"

Nelly nodded happily.

And she waited.

It came to four o'clock and no one was home. Always one of them returned home by then but Richard was supposed to be home sooner. She sat on the floor in front of the door waiting for someone to enter, but when she glanced at the clock and it read half five. (She counted on her fingers).

There was no sign.

Nelly's worrying would lead to more visitors; a few had already been today but she had managed to block them out. The worrying stimulated the drug she had been given, and like a radar, the spirits honed in on her.

Still sitting on the floor, cross legged, she saw the little girl sat opposite her. She smiled. Nelly returned the smile but felt the darkness creep upon her like an evil shadow. She breathed deeper and shut her eyes tightly. Richard had told her to count to ten.

One; two; three.

Something made a creak behind her.

Four; five; six.

Feet pounded along the floor next to her.

Seven; eight; nine.

Someone's breath on her face.

Ten.

Nelly opened her eyes slowly. The little girl was gone. She sighed with relief and clamoured to her feet. She went to her room and reached for the door.

Suddenly an old wrinkled face appeared from behind the door. Her hair was white and her teeth rotten yellow! With a scream, Nelly lashed out and heard the smash of the lamp she had knocked as she sprinted out of the front door. She heard the faint groans from the old woman coming closer and ran down the stairs to the main entrance to the flats. A few others stepped out of their doorways as she bustled past them. She knocked into a few of them and their startled faces frightened her more.

When she reached the open air, her eyes squinted with the sunlight and she continued to stumble down the street like a drunkard.

When Richard and Chloe returned from their evening away, they found an ambulance outside. Richard dropped Chloe's hand like a forgotten toy and rushed inside to check on Nelly. They had spent a romantic evening together but Richard had lost all memory of that when he saw their apartment door was open and their neighbour, Mrs Brown was perched on the sofa with a paramedic nurturing a cut on her forehead.

"W-w-where?" he asked, unable to think of a complete sentence.

Mrs Brown looked up at him, with an almost judgemental expression. "She ran away. I heard someone yelling so I came in to see if everything was alright because Miss

Caddy explained that you would be late this evening and for me to keep an eye on things."

"I see." Richard nodded, quite vigorously considering his next move. But when he saw Chloe enter the flat with an innocent appearance, he nudged her as he passed, knowing it was her fault this had happened.

On the street he walked round endlessly for her. It was dark so was hard to see, but as he was about to give up and return home to wait until daylight, he heard someone crying quietly. He looked down by some nearby steps leading up to a similar building that he lived in and saw some bare feet poking out from under the stairs.

"Nell?" he called gently. "Is that you?"

The whimpering stopped and her whited blonde hair appeared with a tear stained complexion. "Doc?" she grunted.

"Yes it's me. It's Richard." He held out his hand as he crouched next to her. "It's alright Nelly, take my hand."

She hesitated.

"I trust you." He said offering his hand again. She clasped his hand lightly and they stood together, until he managed to put his arm around her. "I've got you."

They returned to the flats, which by now had been emptied of people, including old Mrs Brown. Chloe had fallen asleep of the sofa while waiting for Richard to return. He didn't wake her.

Instead he took Nelly to her room and tucked her in. "I'm sorry," she said.

"You didn't know," he replied.

In his own bed he contemplated his next steps. Nelly, or better known as Patient 2.5.7, was important to him but he couldn't take care of her all his life; especially if he plans to start a proper family with Chloe. He knew Chloe already had ideas. By next morning, he had made his decision.

Chapter Eleven: Goodbye for a Little While

The next morning, Richard woke before Chloe. He helped Nelly wake up and gave her clothes to wear for going out. He took Chloe's car keys and backed a bag.

"Where are we going Richard?" Nelly asked as she looked out of the car window.

"I want you to meet someone," he answered her with not much information.

"Who?"

"Someone you knew a long time ago."

The rest of the way, they drove in silence, but Nelly was happy. She watched out the window and grabbing Richard's arm when she saw something of interest to her. Finally Richard slowed and pulled up in front of a terrace house. Nelly recognised it, but couldn't be sure from where.

As he gave a shove of the rusty gate, Nelly followed Richard cautiously. She had dreams of this place. They waited for someone to answer the door.

Nelly's heart dropped as she saw her mother appear in the window. She knew who it was instantly. The door was opened soon after and they went inside.

"Thank you for seeing us," Richard said with courtesy.

Nelly's mother nodded as a greeting and sat on one of the chairs in the living room. Nelly joined Richard on the opposing sofa.

"I wanted to introduce you to your daughter." Nelly attempted a smile but she remembered the last look her mother gave her before leaving her in Gravehill. It haunted her memories.

"Doctor Pearce has told me about your life in Gravehill," Nelly's mother sounded nervous. "I'm sorry."

Richard tried to reconcile the bond between mother and daughter but it had been too long it seemed. Nelly struggled to speak while her mother continued to be aloof. As half an hour past, Richard explained that Nelly needed a home to feel secure in. Although Nelly was naïve and often confused, she knew what he meant. He wasn't going to do as he promised anymore.

In that moment, Nelly's senses weakened all for her sight. She felt alone again. She saw her mother shake her head and wave her arms sideways. She mentioned her husband. She saw Richard shake his head in a pleading motion and with a few rounds of this, the two stood up. Nelly followed their direction.

She had not looked into her mother's face since she had been there and decided to take one last look at the woman who had given birth to her. Her Mother's mouth moved up and down. She could lip read what she was saying. It was sorry. Sorry sorry sorry. Nelly couldn't understand what she was sorry for all of a sudden. Was it leaving her in the asylum? Was it not loving her? Both she and Richard walked in silence as they got to the car. She turned back and saw a man watching in an upstairs window. When their eyes met, he turned away. That was the last time she was to see her father or her mother.

"I'm sorry Nelly," Richard said kindly. "I thought she might want to see you."

"That's alright." Nelly stared out the window. "Where are you taking me now?"

"Listen, Nelly," Richard faltered. "You need to be in a place that you can be safe and have routine. I can't give you that. Chloe and I cannot give you that."

"I know."

Richard took Nelly to a Home. It wasn't technically a hospital but a place with carers and nurses that mainly helped the aged. When they arrived, Richard took the case he had stashed in the car with them to the reception. A lady welcomed them.

"It's nice to meet you Eleanor," she said with a typical smile. "Shall I take you to your room?"

Nelly nodded, but as Richard began to proceed with them, Nelly stopped him. "This is goodbye then," she said softly.

"No, I'll be here all the time to visit you. I promise." Richard's voice broke as he spoke. He tried to hold back tears as he watched Nelly walk away. It wasn't until he reached the car that he broke down into tears. He would never be sure if this was the right decision, but he didn't want to lose her and this was the best way to make certain of that.

The lady opened a door into a room that was quaint, with a desk and chairs as well as a niceish bed. The window even had curtains. "Here we are then Eleanor," the lady smiled again. "Dinner is at seven and breakfast is at nine in the morning, so make sure you come down for your meals. Is there anything you need?"

"No thank you," Nelly sat on the bed. "Oh, but my name isn't Eleanor." They lady was curious. "Call me 2.5.7." She lifted her sleeve and revealed her arm band, with the three numbers printed on it.

The lady nodded sympathetically and shut the door as she left. Nelly looked around the room for a moment and placed the blanket over herself. She was home; in a room with little space like she was used to. She held herself and felt the band of cloth on her arm, rubbing it gently. "Yes" she said to herself. "I'm safe; in room 2.5.7."

Chapter Twelve: 1958 – A Year Apart Forever in my Heart

Richard had been working for almost a year in this hospital until he heard his patient's name once again. He had become accustomed to his routine of work that was generically uninteresting compared with his previous work. He came home every day to Chloe, who continued to work her own shifts in a separate hospital. She also, quite obviously, hinted marriage to Richard, who seemed more oblivious than ever. His mind would often wander to his patient, especially on quiet nights; and he couldn't help but take a moment in her old room to consider her lonely existence in the home he and Chloe had placed her. Chloe pretended not to notice his behaviour. She had been adamant it was the right decision for them all, but Richard suffered silently.

One particular day in which Richard's life would soon merge with his patient's again, he heard a man call out his name. In his workplace, it was not unusual for his name to be called but as the voice rang through his ears, he knew his next few decisions were going to be important.

"Doctor Pearce," the voice announced. As he turned in the voice's direction, Richard saw a man holding out a badge of identification, while making his way towards him. My name is detective Frank Smith. I was hoping to talk with you about a former patient of yours."

"Of course" Richard's heart leapt into his throat. He dared not to consider it to be his patient he wished it to be out of fear of disappointment. He took the detective to a small office.

"It's about Eleanor Walton. Do you remember-"

"Yes." Richard heard his own eagerness within his voice.

"Good. We are investigating the murder of Doctor De Ville. He was found in the rubble of the Gravehill Asylum."

"That burnt down a year ago! He's only just been found?"

"He had been found earlier than this but it wasn't until recently that we found evidence that he died before the flames reached his body."

"And why do you think Ne- I mean Patient 2.5.7 would have anything to do with it?"

"Patient 2.5.7 was the last scheduled patient to have a consultation with him. It is also on her records that she had killed before."

Richard paused for a moment; he tried to think fast. "I don't see how I can help with this?"

The detective was more tentative. "Well we've tried to see the patient before, but she can be difficult. I was hoping you could attend some interviews as her representative to help her understand?"

Richard agreed, although it concerned him to see her again. It wasn't due to safety or by awkwardness of sending her to the home in the first place; it was his feelings he was afraid of. He never allowed himself to feel as he wanted to feel. He couldn't let himself. After packing his doctor case, he and the detective took a drive to the home he had dropped her off those many months ago.

The memories flooded back to him. The image of her sad expression pushed to the front of his mind as they drove up to the front door. He felt sick. Although the place was a lot different than that of Gravehill, his overwhelming guilt swamped his nerves with shakes. The patients within this place were mainly elderly with ailing illnesses. As they entered a nurse had been waiting for them and took them straight to Nelly's room. Richard's heart pounded. They found Nelly with another nurse, playing cards.

When his eyes met hers, Richard felt the electricity spark within him like it never had gone away in the first place. He saw her eyes fixate on him as both he and the detective entered the room.

The detective attempted an introduction but Nelly had already moved to Richard's side. She didn't touch him. He didn't either, no matter how much he wanted to. He wanted to hold her, just for a moment; just to make sure she was real.

The nurse called Nelly to sit down again and Richard also took a seat. She had been named 2.5.7, he didn't like that.

"Hello Eleanor," the detective spoke gently. "Do you remember that I've visited before?"

"Yes." She was still looking at Richard.

"Do you remember Doctor Pearce?"

"Yes." Her tone was deadening. "Doctor Richard Pearce."

"He is helping me with the investigation about Doctor De Ville." As she did not answer him, Richard requested a moment alone with his former patient. The detective allowed it and both he and the two nurses left the room for a moment.

"Are they treating you alright?" Richard asked moving his hand across the table so it was resting just a millimetre away from hers.

"I am fine?" she moved away remembering he had left her there. "You promised you would visit."

"I know."

"You did not visit."

"I know." Richard's remorseful tone was heard on deafened ears as Nelly couldn't understand why he had not done what he had said he was going to do. He took a moment before remembering he had an important reason for being there. He reminded her of the night of the fire, but Nelly didn't need it. She had nightmares of it every night. He told her to be honest about how Doctor De Ville treated her and to explain that she had manage to get out of the fire with Richard and Chloe the first time.

"I didn't though?" she questioned. "You came back for me?"

"You just need to say it the way I have explained and trust me."

The detective returned to the room with questions that Richard thought he might ask and like a good girl she answered the questions well and lied about escaping the fire with Richard and Chloe.

"Thank you Eleanor," the detective stated as he wrote his final note on her writing pad. He stood up and passed Richard as he moved. He was sure he would native the bead of sweat that ran down his forehead. "I'm sorry I have to do this but I am arresting you for the suspected murder of Doctor De Ville."

"WHAT!!?" Richard stood quickly trying to stop the handcuffs being placed on Nelly's wrists.

"Doctor please." The detective pushed Richard aside. "We have the evidence we need." He noticed the stress on Richard's face. "Or would you like me to look into your file with more detail?"

Richard released his grip on the detective. They gave Patient 2.5.7 a strong sedative as she tried to resist and the detective explained that she would remain here so not to disrupt her routine too much. Richard saw the distress in her face as he was escorted with the detective, off the premises. He went home and as the detective dropped him off, he stated that Richard may be needed during the court proceedings. Richard didn't even blink in his direction.

He placed his key in the lock and pushed the door with a light shove, greeted by Chloe, who hadn't notice his daze. She wrapped her arms around him and kissed him passionately on the neck. He didn't react.

She talked and talked about things Richard had no interest in and he remained in his trance. Finally he stopped her. "I saw Nelly today."

"Who?" she questioned with disinterest.

"Patient 2.5.7."

"Oh." Her voice and posture changed. She moved away from him and sat on the other chair.

He explained the investigation and the lie he had told during the fire. Chloe was not comfortable with it. She didn't want to lie for her. The conversation lasted until bed in which Chloe stated firmly that they were to have nothing more to do with it since Patient 2.5.7 was nothing to do with them anymore.

As she snored lightly, Richard laid wide awake with his eyes open, thinking about his patient trapped or even encased within that home he had forced her into. He had given her that life. He could have made her life so much more if he hadn't been a coward. He knew that.

Suddenly, he felt his bladder pull him out of bed. After flushing the loo, he found himself getting dressed and putting his shoes on. Grabbing Chloe's car keys and packing some clothes, he made his way to the home.

It was night time so security was not at its strength. He glided through reception and found Nelly's room; locked.

Thrusting his body into the door, he caught sight of a snoozing Nelly who was feeling the effects of the sedative. Still with the handcuffs on her wrists, Richard propped Nelly over his shoulder and they rushed through the corridors. Nelly woke enough to move on her own. She didn't want to touch him, but she had to.

Security had been alerted by the bang of the door and were hot on their tails, but they reached the car in time, where Richard slammed his foot onto the accelerator and with a screech, they sped off.

"Stay awake, just stay awake," Richard chanted to Nelly as she did her best to keep her eyes open. They eventually reached a public car park that was about twenty minutes from a train station. The car was dumped as Richard beckoned Nelly to follow him. He had two cases in his hands. She stumbled behind him with bare feet and still in her sheet-like night dress.

Just before they came to the turning for the station, Richard removed his coat and wrapped it around Nelly so she wouldn't stand out too much. He sat her down on a bench as he arranged everything. The whole process took time.

The train finally arrived about a half hour later. Nelly had rested her head on Richard's shoulder and fallen asleep. She was snoring lightly. Richard shifted in his seat a little and lightly touched Nelly's knee. She twitched awake and moved away from him. She apologised nervously. He half smiled just for being close to her.

"Our train is here," Richard said offering his arm to assist her, but she didn't want to touch him. As she followed him, she tried to pull her sleeves up so she could use her hands. Richard's overcoat was too big for her. She tripped a couple of times while finding an empty carriage and eventually Richard chose one. He placed the cases on top of the seating shelves and offered her place by the window.

She sat and he checked the corridor, before making himself comfortable next to her. He noticed her eyes were heavy and bloodshot. "Are you tired?"

"A little bit," she replied.

"Have a rest now, I'll wake you when it's time to move," he explained as he stroked her hair so lightly that he was hardly touching her. "Are you warm enough?"

Nelly yawned and nodded lightly. She fell asleep almost straight away.

It was a long journey. Richard sat in silence all the way. He was unsure of where he was going to go; life on the run did not seem the best decision with someone who has never seen real life before. The train was taking them south and he decided to take another train to his childhood home. It was a little village in Wales; a village that most people would have never heard of. He thought it was the best decision as he could only trust one person and she lived in his village.

On the following train, his mind wandered to Chloe. He felt guilty for leaving her without saying goodbye. They had left things broken after that argument. He hoped she would understand.

By the time they got into the station, it was very late. There were no buses running this late and the village was still quite a long way off. Richard helped Nelly onto the platform and they watched as the train chugged away. Richard shivered. It was a cold night. He tugged at Nelly's sleeve and walked closely next to him. She was still very tired.

"It's about two miles this way, and then we'll be safe." Richard moved onward and Nelly dragged her feet behind him. He was feeling tired too but tried to hold himself strong for Nelly's sake.

By the time they reached the village it was nearing midnight and all the little houses were dark and quiet. It had been raining so the fallen leaves were slippery. He was careful not to tread on any big clumps. He was aware that if they were to make too much noise it would cause villagers to see them.

The village itself was within two hills. They had started at the top of one and were passing the old church in the centre of town in the dip of the hills. It became harder to walk up the hill, as he felt Nelly slip further and further away from him. He stopped himself from walking too far ahead, afraid of losing her.

Suddenly he heard a thump. Nelly had fallen. He dropped the cases he was carrying and hurried to her. On lifting her chin, he saw her exhausted, wet face. It had started to rain. It was going to take a while for her to get over the drugs she had been given.

He lifted her in his arms and strode to where he had dropped the cases. "We're almost there Nelly?" he whispered.

"Sorry," she replied weakly.

"There is nothing to be sorry for!" he said trying to pick up a case while still handling her. Instead, he pushed it with his foot, and then the other case. Slowly he reached a row of terrace houses on the left halfway up the hill. He counted the forth one along and stopped at the gate.

It was hard to see but he knew the house had not changed since he was last there. He lifted Nelly a little higher over the stone wall and she leaned against it. After shaking his arms loose, he picked up the cases and went through the gate. The small garden was still bushy although it was autumn.

He crouched by the door and looked under a number of pots surrounding the path.

All of the sudden a light had been switched on within the house. He heard a voice from inside. "I have a gun and I can use it! My husband was a Captain you know!"

"Mother!" he murmured harshly. "Mam it's me!"

"Me who?" The door opened ajar, still with the chain on.

"Rick?"

"I do not know any *Rick*!"

"Mum. Open the door."

The door opened and standing in the doorway was an older woman nearing fifty with a nightgown and dressing gown on. Her hair had been tied in ribbons but seemed a little greyer than when he had seen her last. "My little boy!" She grabbed his face and kissed him for a moment, and on the release of her grip she gave him a good slap. "You stupid boy! It is ridiculously late!"

"I'm sorry Mum! Stop hitting me!" He pulled her arms off him and held them as he spoke again. "I need your help."

She gave him a caring nod and he turned back to his patient still resting against the stone wall. He saw his mother's expression as he lifted Nelly in his arms and took her inside. His mother gestured the sofa, which he rested her on. His mother brought the case in and asked who the woman was, but Richard avoided the question.

"We can put her in the guest room," she decided, "I want to bath her feet first though. No shoes?"

Richard did not answer, but hurried to the kitchen, grabbing a cloth and a bowl filled with water. "Here Mum."

She dabbed the young woman's cut feet gently but it didn't seem to bother her. She was out cold. As Richard was taking Nelly upstairs, she spoke again. "But Richard, I want to know who this woman is, so I expect you to tell me in the morning."

He nodded and grunted like a little boy would to his mother when in trouble.

The guest room was small but cosy. Richard took his overcoat off Nelly and revealed her white sheet-like garment. He heard his mother gasp from the doorway.

"Do we have anything she could wear Mum?" he asked as he undid the string from her neck and loosened her clothing. His mother placed a nightgown at the bottom of the bed and noticed how her son looked at the patient. He turned to his mother, "It might be best if you-".

"Of course," she said kindly and rubbed his back thoughtfully. "Your bed is already made so you go off to bed. I'll make sure she sleeps alright."

"But Mum she-"

"Different? I gathered. She's got a fever and only Mum's can deal with these sorts of illnesses, not doctors." She smiled and sat on the edge of the bed. His heart warmed as he watched his mother care for Nelly. "Oh and Richard, You're a good boy." He went straight to bed and slept the whole night. He felt safe at home. He'd forgotten what it felt like.

As his mother wiped the patient's brow, Nelly awoke and glimpsed at her. "Hello dear, my name is Patricia, what is yours?" Nelly smiled weakly. She lifted her left hand and put up two fingers then all five. She fell asleep again before she could say anything. Patricia, with a confused frown took off the woman's clothes gently. The sheet-like clothing was coarse and thin. Patricia thought about putting it in the bin but decided against it just in case. Her nightgown was larger than the woman so was quite baggy and easy to slip on.

Patricia lifted Nelly's left side and realised she still had a piece of cloth on her left arm. She tried to pull it off but it did not budge from the under part of the arm. She realised there was writing on it. "Two five seven?" she questioned a loud.

Suddenly, Nelly grabbed her arm tightly and Patricia was pulled closer to her. Patricia felt a small shooting pain on the side of her head and saw a vision of white walls and numbers. The vision flickered in her mind like flashing pictures. She was taken to a room and a doctor was stood waiting for her. When she moved out of the way, a little girl had come into the room. Her hair was white.

The scene became fuzzy and after a few seconds, Patricia saw the girl lying on the surgical bed. The nurse was clamping her head to the bed with a metal brace. She did the same to the little girl's hands and feet. The doctor hovered over her and Patricia could feel the little girl's fear like it was her own. She looked about six or seven.

As the scene became blurred again, Patricia rubbed her eyes within the dream and saw a nurse come into the room with a metal plate. It had a piece of cloth and a needle and thread. She gave it to the doctor, who threaded the surgical needle and lifted it to the light as if to check it was clean.

Patricia felt a pain in the pit of her stomach. She didn't want to see it. She didn't even want know about it. She couldn't look away. The needle punctured the skin several times and blood oozed out like dripping taps. There was no anaesthetic and the little girl's screams resonated within the room like a howling wolf's. The nurse was holding her down tightly; so much so that the little was bruising on her shoulders, where she was leaning.

When the doctor was done, the nurse mopped the blood that had made a puddle on the floor. She then dabbed the wound. Patricia moved closer to the girl to see her face. Her face was blotchy and her eyes were still filled with tears. The doctor assisted her up and explained that it will hurt for a while.

When the little girl stood up, Patricia felt how weak she was. She swayed with emotion. Then she saw the number, which confirmed her suspicion. On the cloth it read 2.5.7 and the doctor said, “Ok we’re going to take you to your room now, Patient 2.5.7.”

As he spoke his words, Patricia zoned back into her guest bedroom and the woman in the bed had released her grip. She held her head and looked down and the woman in the bed. After a moment of caution she lifted the woman’s arm again and found it still sewn into her arm. The thread had imbedded itself within her skin from the years it had been in place. It had bled a number of times over the years, judging by the stains. As she stared at the old wound, she carefully slipped on the nightgown. Nelly had a number of scars all over her body, but that underarm scar was by far the worst. Patricia’s mind fixated on the numbers; these numbers, she was never going to forget. Even when she went to her own bed, those numbers stayed with her like a bad smell. As she laid in her bed thinking, an overwhelming smell of blood flooded her nostrils. The metallic rotting scent made her feel queasy and Patricia ran to the bathroom. She threw up.

“Are you alright Mum?” Richard was standing in the doorway, as Patricia was slumped over the toilet.

“Yes son, sorry.” She flushed the toilet and washed her hands in the sink.

“Did anything happen?” Richard took the towel that was resting on the bath edge and helped his Mum dry her hands and face.

“That girl in there, I know who she is.”

“Who?”

“That poor woman’s name is Patient 2.5.7 and the pain she’s been through.” She shook her head. “She needs love Richard. And we are going to give it to her!”

Chapter Thirteen: Start of a Beautiful Friendship

Nelly blinked awake and yawned never endingly. She sat up and adapted to her surroundings as she couldn't remember where she was and how she got there. The room was a warm blue with flowery curtains. Looking at the nightgown she was wearing, she waddled out of the room slowly and found the stairs leading downwards. Her feet were very sore and she tried to avoid treading on the balls of her feet. There were noises coming from downstairs. When she reached the ground floor, Patricia smiled at her kindly; her wrinkles highlighting her smile.

"Well a good morning to you my dear!" she said cheerfully. Nelly didn't reply. "Come and have some breakfast." Patricia pointed at a seat, which took Nelly to the table seated. She placed a fry up in front of her and Nelly just stared at it. There was a lot of food. "My name is Patricia, but you can call me Pat, do you remember?"

"No sorry," Nelly's voice was croaky.

"What do I call you?" Pat's voice shook with the thought of the numbers. She noticed Nelly touch her left arm, as if confirming her own identity.

"Um," she hesitated. "Doctor Pearce calls me Nelly."

"And I shall too." Pat smiled with relief. "Eat up. Richard will be back in a few minutes. He popped out to speak with the milkman."

Nelly picked up a fork that had been neatly placed next to the plate of food. Holding it like a child, she stabbed the chunks of sausage already cut for her and chewed slowly. She was enjoying it.

The front door opened and Pat watched her guest flinch like a frightened rabbit. Her son's eyes lit up when he saw them. He plonked the two bottles of milk on the table and sat down with them. "You're up!" he grinned.

"We've been introduced." Pat confirmed to him. "Nelly and I are becoming acquainted."

"I see," he turned to Nelly. "Did she actually tell you who she is?" Nelly shook her head. "She's my mum."

Nelly noticed how he resembled his mother and watched the connection they had. It made her think of her own mother. "Oh," she said nervously.

"What's wrong?" Pat leaned towards her.

"Nothing." Nelly's hand was shaking as she hovered the fork over her plate of food.

"Pat wants you here Nell, so don't worry." Richard explained and turned his direction to his mother, "she has a strained relationship with her family."

"Ok," Pat stood up and poured a glass of orange juice for Nelly. She stoked Nelly's head as she passed, feeling her flinch again.

Over the next couple of days, Nelly was introduced to the family home and routine. Pat would do the washing, cleaning and cooking, while Richard visited his friends and kept an eye on Nelly.

Finally after about a week, Richard took a job with his friend at a farm that was near the village. Pat never asked about why he came home with a patient and took a step back in his career. She felt it wasn't her place to know, although she was desperate to find out. She often asked Nelly questions to see what she knew, but it was never the full story.

Pat would often sit with Nelly while she slept due to her night terrors. Richard didn't want to explain the abnormalities attached to his patient for fear his mother wouldn't believe him.

Eventually, Nelly became more confident in taking part in discussions and she was always excited for Richard to come home so she could learn what he did during the day. She was stuck at home, with strict instructions from Richard not to be left her on her own for too long.

On a particular day, about a month after her arrival, Pat came home from the pouring rain. She was soaked through. She removed her hat and coat, and called for Nelly. Nelly walked into the living room slowly and carefully. She was holding a cup and saucer.

Pat smiled and sat herself down on the sofa. "It's raining cats and dogs out there my darling!" she said. Nelly gave her the cup. "What's this then?"

"Tea," she settled next to her. "I wanted to show my um,"

"Appreciation?"

"Yes that's it!" she confirmed with a pointed finger. "I wanted to show my apprec-iation? And I know you always drink tea. I've turned the fire off as well."

Pat chuckled. "You mean the hob my sweetheart." She took a sip.

"Is it alright?"

"Perfect because you made it." Pat rubbed Nelly's back and kissed her on the head. She placed her cup of tea on the side table and searched for her cigarettes, finding them under her bag that she had plonked on the other table. Happily, she lit her cigarette. "Why don't you have a look in my shopping bag by the front door," she puffed. Nelly's eyes narrowed with suspicion and after bringing the bag over, she removed the wrapped items. Pat insisted on her opening the items. She noticed how gentle and careful she was to not break the brown paper.

"Clothes?" Nelly looked up.

"Well I'm fed up of you borrowing mine and making me feel fat as they hang off you," she joked. Nelly hesitated at first but realised she was joking and joined in with her laughter. She ordered her to put her new outfit on and for her to come down and help to make dinner.

When Nelly returned from her bedroom to the kitchen, she was wearing a new outfit. It was a two piece with a white top with buttons and a tanned coloured skirt. As she ran down the stairs with excitement and into the kitchen, she skidded to a halt.

"You look beautiful Nelly," Pat said but she realised something was wrong when she caught Nelly's expression. "What is it Nell?"

Nelly stood still staring in the corner of the kitchen. A man wearing dark clothes was standing covered in dirt. "I can't say," Nelly replied. The man lifted his heavy head and looked at Nelly. His bloodshot eyes were stern and blood seeped from his mouth as he tried to speak.

Nelly had tears running down her cheeks and as Pat tried to comfort her, she lashed out and pushed her away, choking. She could feel her throat becoming more and more fiery. She felt blood surging from her innards to her mouth. "I'm bleeding I'm bleeding," she screamed repeatedly.

"Nelly I can't see anything!"

Nelly gagged like she was throwing up the blood that she could feel. Suddenly she felt a sharp pain in her stomach. She looked at the man as she fell to her knees. He was also clutching his stomach. He had been stabbed. Nelly began screaming with the pain and as she blinked she saw the man coming closer to her. "No!"

The man leaned over her and he pressed his finger where he had been stabbed. The pain was unbearable. She wanted to stop!

Pat had been helpless trying to calm her but failing. When Nelly starting shaking uncontrollably on the floor, Pat filled up a bowl of cold water and threw it over Nelly, just as she saw her eyes roll back.

The sharp cold water pricked Nelly's senses and she stopped fitting. In the panic of it all, Pat threw another bowl of cold water over her and this time it wakened her. Nelly took a breath in and shivered – her eyes open wide in shock. With shortness of breath, Nelly sat up and Pat clutched her tightly. She squeezed her tightly rocking her gently.

"It's alright Nelly, I've got you." Pat heard the front door open and close. Richard was home.

When he saw both his Mum and Nelly on the kitchen floor, he rushed to them. "What's happened?!" he gulped.

"I honestly, don't know." Richard could see his mother was scared. He had never seen her like this before.

"I'm sorry," Nelly croaked and both Richard and Pat helped her stand. "Can I change out of these wet clothes?" They let her go upstairs on her own and that gave Richard the chance to explain.

He explained that Nelly had been a patient in Gravehill and that they were on the run. His mum was silent for what felt like a long time while she processed the information.

Finally, she spoke. "So you are telling me that you believe Nelly sees dead people? They just roam around scaring her?"

"I don't know the full ins and outs of it all but I do believe she sees something that is there," Richard paused. "I've seen them too."

"What?" Pat stood up and poured herself a whiskey and soda.

"Mum you don't even like whiskey."

"I need something since my son is losing his mind!" she gulped the drink in one and cringed at the taste. She lit a cigarette.

"I know it sounds mad but you have to believe me!"

They heard a creak and Nelly had returned downstairs and joined them in the living room. She looked better and had put on a different outfit that Pat had bought for her.

"Shall we start dinner then?" Pat decided it best not to bring anything up in front of Nelly. They started making the dinner together with Pat watching carefully while Nelly chopped the vegetables. Richard went for a shower as he was still smelly after the farm.

When he came for dinner, Nelly almost pounced on him with excitement and he couldn't help but take hold of her waist as she bounded towards him. He felt the urge to lift her but suppressed it as he saw his mother's nosey observations.

"Well something smells nice!" he said and noticed that Nelly looked different somehow; more grownup in her new clothes.

They ate at the table and headed to living room to rest. Richard pulled out an old box of photographs, showing Nelly baby pictures of him. The three were enjoying themselves laughing at the bad photographs during Richard's teenage years.

Richard found a picture of his mum with a little girl. He could tell his mother must have been pregnant with him at the time the picture was taken. "Who's this in this one Mum?" Richard asked looking at the picture.

"That's my friend, Laurel," Nelly said.

"No it's not Nelly."

"Yes it is. I'm sure."

Pat leaned forward from sitting on the sofa. "Nelly, you recognise this little girl?"

"Yes."

"This was my daughter." Pat took the photograph. "She died before you were born."

"You never told me that Mam," Richard took his mother's hand.

"It was a long time ago Richard and I don't like to talk about it."

"But how did she die?"

"She drowned," Nelly answered.

Pat with a surprised expression agreed. "How often do you see her?"

"Just sometimes. She usually comes as a warning before others come." Richard suddenly realised why Nelly had seen a little girl with him. It was his sister that he had never met.

"Was she there the last time?" thinking about Nelly's episode in the kitchen earlier.

Richard could see his mother getting ideas that may not be possible, so he decided to stop the conversation. "You'd better be off the bed now Nelly," he stated firmly but kindly.

Nelly stood up from the floor and started for the stairs. "Night Sweet-pea," Pat said and waited for Nelly to be out of earshot. "That's why she's here."

"Mum don't overthink this."

"I'm not, but I want to take Nelly out more. She can't be cooped up in this place all the time."

"Mum you don't understand-"

"I know there are people after her. I know. She needs to understand people so let me help." She stood up from the sofa and stormed off up the stairs.

Richard poured himself a glass of whiskey and took a sip. He knew his mother was right. Turning on the television he watched part of a film that was on. It showed a romantic moment where the man protected his lady. He moved his gaze to the staircase.

In the end he went upstairs and after a bathe he put on his pyjamas that were stripy blue. He saw his mother's light on, but as he went to the door to knock, he hesitated.

"Richard," called a soft voice from the end of the corridor.

"Nell?" he turned to find her standing by her door. "You alright?"

"Yes," she stepped towards him, with her flowing nightdress wafting by her walk. "Are you annoyed because I saw something again?"

"No, no no!" he went to her and smoothed his hands over her bare arms, careful not to touch her arm band. "I just worry about you."

She fiddled with a button on his pyjama shirt. "I want to get better at things Rick," she whispered. "Pat said she wants to take me places."

He took her hand and felt her quiver. He kissed it and replied, "You will." He watched as she returned to her room; her white hair surrounded by a glow of light from the room lamp.

Soon after, Pat had a retired old teacher assist Nelly in writing and reading. Eventually the whole village had met the patient. Pat showed her off like she was a proud mother and there was a lot of gossip about who she was to Richard. It was a known fact that she was a little strange but no one blamed her for it. In fact it made them like her all the more for it.

Richard would often walk arm in arm with her around the village and even took her to the farm a few times to meet the animals. Pat, who was a keen member of the Women's Institute and church goer, had Nelly accompany her to volunteering events like cake sales, but her mind would often wander to thoughts of her first born.

Pat became more and more aware of Nelly's powers. It made her consider the stories Nelly must know, and the things she sees that only she could see. She wanted to know more.

Chapter Fourteen: Time to Let Go

Eight o'clock on a Sunday and Pat stood at the bottom of the steps impatiently. Nelly came running down the stairs and Pat touched up her make up for her.

"Mum, this tie is not working!" Richard groaned as he thumped down the stairs.

"Oh, give it here!" she moaned. She tied it correctly and pushed it tight to his throat. "We'll be late!"

"Mum, we have an hour?"

"Not if we want my seat! Nelly you ready?"

"Um well-"

"Good! Let's go."

They went down the hill and to the church. This was Nelly's first time. It was an old church made of stone, with a large clock on its steeple. A graveyard surrounded it with the newer ones closer to the path leading to the old oak door.

Pat rushed on ahead to meet the vicar, who was standing by the door. He was thanking her for doing the flowers.

Nelly reached the metal gates that were at the boundary of the church grounds. She stopped. Richard who had been walking beside her turned to her. He saw tears in her eyes. He tried to speak to her but his voice was lost by her own fear of what she could see. When Richard looked in the direction she did he saw graves and his mother and vicar in the distance. But Nelly saw things that he couldn't. Over one hundred people stood amongst the headstones. All pale skinned and staring at their own graves.

Richard tugged Nelly to come with him. "I can't," she whispered. "They'll see me."

"I'm right her Nelly. Nothing can harm you." Richard took her hand and they walked slowly through the boundary. Nelly heard her step inside like an echo and she saw the people turn and look at her. They were talking. They wanted something. She felt them run through her body like bad chills and she faltered every time. They knew she could see them.

Even Richard felt the strain from her reaction. It was not right. He pulled her close to him in an attempt to stop her feeling their forces.

Pat turned back to them as she was standing with the vicar. She realised Nelly was struggling. She paced to her and took her other arm while Richard had the other.

"Do you see Laurel?" Pat asked.

Nelly looked around. "There are too many," she whispered. "She doesn't stay if more come." They reached the church and went inside. The church was filled, with no room to sit down. Nelly halted and waited for Richard to catch up with her as he had been stopped by the vicar.

Pat was with her and said "Oh good, we're first," seeing the church empty and prepared for this morning's parishioners. She went to the fifth row and took a seat. Nelly shook as she watched her sit making the person she could see, already sat there, disappear. She took a seat next to her. She shivered. "It's always cold in here." Pat realised Nelly did not look well. She felt woozy and the cold chill that ran through her did not help matters. "These souls Nelly, try and speak to them. If you help them, they might be less scary." Pat touched her arm in a bid to calm her, but instead felt Nelly's emotions. She heard the voices talking. They were loud and repetitive; all talking at once. It gave Pat a headache, just hearing them for a few seconds. Retracting her arm she called Richard, who came quickly and joined them.

"Richard, Nelly isn't well."

"I know Mum."

Nelly's eyes became bloodshot and she watched many souls standing by the alter. She couldn't comprehend what they were saying. There was too many of them. Then she saw her; that little girl. She had not seen her in a while. Her hair was just as brown and just as wet as the other times she had seen her last. Her hearing had deafened the others around her.

"Mummy," she whispered. It wasn't her voice.

Pat turned to her. She recognised the voice immediately.

"Mummy, are you there Mummy?"

"Laurel?" Pat wheezed. Her hands came to her mouth and tears ran down her cheeks.

"You can't see me Mummy but I'm wet and cold."

"Mum," Richard interrupted. "What's going on?"

"We need to go." She hissed. She stood and made her apologies to the vicar. Richard turned Nelly's head and saw her spaced expression. He tapped her face and like something came out of her, she was Nelly again. He took her home.

Pat was already there. She had a cigarette in the side of her mouth and a glass of straight vodka in her hand. Richard helped Nelly sit on the sofa, who was weakened by the event.

He went in the kitchen to his mother. "Mum? What happened?"

"What is she?" Pat swallowed her drink in one and leaned on the kitchen counter.

"Mum! Are you drinking?" he smelt the glass. "It's eight thirty in the morning!"

"Answer me!" she screamed.

"I don't know!" he shouted back. He took a deep breath. "She knows things that's all. She sees certain things."

"Sees what?" Pat poured another glass. "Because that was not her voice she was speaking in that church!"

"Mum you need to calm down! We've been through this."

"I know that! But I was not expecting that!" she raised her voice again. "You bring a mental patient to my house and I am to accept it when she starts knowing things about my own life. And speaking like my Laurel." Her voice choked at the end of her sentence.

"What did she do wrong?"

"She sounded just like Laurel." She repeated herself.

"Pat," Nelly whispered.

"I just need to get my head round this."

"Pat," Nelly spoke louder.

"My head is splitting!"

Suddenly, the room began to shake. Nelly screamed! It was high pitched and short. Richard and Pat rushed into the living room and as they lost their balance, they watched Nelly shaking uncontrollably. Pat gripped the side of her sofa and pulled herself towards Nelly. She grabbed her. She squeezed her arms tightly until she found the energy and the balance to hold her. "Patricia!" Nelly shouted. She stood up and grabbed her by her head, pressing her thumbs on Pat's temples and putting her head against hers.

The earthquake stopped and Pat felt the flickering sensation she had felt when she had the vision the night she arrived. She was taken back to her own memories. They were walking along a river bank. They being Pat, her husband and little Laurel. They were laughing and Laurel was running ahead of them. Heavily pregnant, Pat rested on a bench, leaving Laurel and her husband to go on ahead.

All of a sudden the vision took a turn. It wasn't a memory anymore. Nelly was leading her to the scene she never got to see. Her mind went further along the river bank and she saw her husband trip and fall. But as he gathered his balance, Laurel had already been playing too close to the bank and she fell in. Pat called but no one could hear her; she wasn't really there. In moments she drowned further down the river.

"It wasn't anyone's fault Mummy," Laurel said as the vision had shifted to their house. They were generic scenes that were of times gone by – Sunday dinners, birthdays, anniversaries. Laurel was there each time, but Pat could never see her. And each time she was there, she would say that it wasn't anyone's fault. She was even there when Pat broke down into tears.

Finally, Pat was alone with the ghost of her daughter. She ran to her and hugged her tight. "My baby," Pat cried.

"Can I go now Mummy?" Laurel said. "It was no one's fault."

"Of course you can my sweetheart," Pat sniffed. "Just know that I love you, I've never stopped loving you."

"I know Mummy. I told Nelly you would look after her, since her Mummy never wanted her."

"Is that why Richard found her?"

"I like my little brother. He used to see me too but then one day he stopped. He grew. Nelly never stopped seeing me and I wanted her to be happy. I thought she would make you happy too."

"She does."

"Good. So if I go you will be alright now?"

"Yes."

"I love you Mummy."

"I love you too."

Pat's vision was fading and she began feeling Nelly's thumbs against her temples again. She opened her eyes, where her mascara had run. "Is she gone?" she whispered to Nelly.

"Yes, she's gone."

"Thank you." She replied and with tears in her eyes held onto Nelly in a firm clasp. She turned to Richard and saw him struggle to his feet. He had not regained his balance from the shaking. He took a deep breath.

"I don't want to see them but I do," Nelly explained.

"I know my darling. I know." And she did know; not fully; but she did believe that she had a gift she needed to learn control. They never mentioned what happened again. But Pat and Nelly became a lot closer. Nelly was learning and becoming more confident. She was even beginning to understand the people that visited her. Pat told her to focus on each one individually and not let them take over. In a way, Richard and Nelly had forgotten they were in hiding. They were beginning to lead a normal life and Richard had almost forgotten his fiancé.

Chapter Fifteen: Nelly's First Birthday

On an autumn day, Nelly had been round Mr Price's house practicing her reading before taking his dog for his usual walk. She had become accustomed to her Tuesday routine. In conversation, Nelly had let it slip it was her birthday that day. Mr Price was surprised and wished her well. As soon as she left, he rang Pat to inform her.

Nelly made her way up the hill and as soon as she came through the front door, Pat gave her a big hug and kiss saying happy birthday. Nelly didn't want to have the fuss Pat was prepared to make. She wasn't used to it. The day always made her sad.

"I've got you a little something for the occasion!" Pat squealed with excitement.

"That was quick!" Nelly said. "I don't need anything honestly. It's just a normal day to me."

"I got these ages ago as I wasn't sure when your birthday was going to be and I like to be prepared." She revealed a two boxes tied with ribbons. "Open. Open! Open!"

The bigger box contained a maroon coloured dress with a V-neck and fell to the knee. The smaller box contained matching shoes. "They're beautiful," Nelly gasped. "I've never had anything so lovely. Thank you Pat."

Pat smiled and kissed her on top of her head again. "Well I'm off to get a cake! Back now in a minute," she called as she rushed out grabbing her coat along the way. Nelly dressed herself in the clothes Pat had so kindly bought for her. She slumped onto the sofa and rested her eyes after twirling around in her beautiful clothes. She was wakened by the front door slamming again. It was Richard.

"Sorry did I wake you?" he said smiling.

"I was just resting." Nelly sat up and leaned onto the back of the sofa. "What's that?" There was a basket on the floor.

"I thought you might be hungry and it's quite a nice day?" He picked the basket up and took Nelly's coat from the hanger. Nelly sighed wanting to stay inside but Richard wasn't having any of it. "Come on Lazy, and don't forget your shoes this time."

"One time!" Nelly moaned smiling and stood up straightening her dress.

Richard's eyes brightened as he saw her standing. "Wait," he said.

She stood still like she had accidentally stood in something. "What?"

"You look very pretty today," he said. She thanked him and placed her coat on. He helped of course. They went outside to see the autumn leaves falling and the crisp breeze blowing them around. Richard took Nelly up the top of the hill which was the villages end and laid a blanket on the grass. He had brought pasties and finger sandwiches. They took a while munching on the food and

Richard constantly made silly jokes to make her laugh. He became a little nervous for some reason.

Richard rested his hand on the blanket and caught Nelly's as he did so. Both of them glanced down. "I want to thank you Rick, for being so nice to me." She shifted closer to him and he gazed at her as her hair blew in the breeze.

"And I should say Happy Birthday," he smiled smoothing his hand over hers.

"You know," she said disappointed.

"There's nothing wrong knowing these things. And anyway; I should thank you."

"Why?"

Richard moved closer to her and brushed her hair out of her face with his hand. "Because you always make me happy. There's something about you. There always has been Nell, even when I only knew you as 2.5.7."I want to show you something," she said leaning onto her knees. He saw flashes of her birthdays throughout her life. She was alone in everyone; in her room; alone. He leaned in closer to her as his hand was placed on her neck. She placed her hand over his and kissed it gently. He tended towards her to kiss her, but she jerked away nervously.

"I'm scared Richard," she quivered. "I don't want to hurt you."

"Let me take the risk Nelly." He puckered his lips to hers and was millimetres away. Their eyes shut and he smoothed her back and she felt his chest. They were almost connected.

Nelly blinked and in the corner of her eye she saw someone. She twitched as she recognised the person watching them.

"What is it?"

"De Ville is here!" she whispered moving away from Richard.

"He's dead." As he spoke he realised what he had said meant nothing in Nelly's case. He looked around. He saw someone in the distance for a brief second but he thought it must be his mind playing tricks on him. There would be no one out that far at this time. "We'd better go back then." There was disappointment in his voice. He helped her stand and packed everything away. They didn't say anything as they walked back. Nelly felt strange seeing Doctor De Ville again, but Richard felt it was a subconscious sign that Nelly did not feel the same way as he did. It was a way of avoiding the subject.

Nelly used her key to open the front door and as she walked through a group of people shouted "SURPRISE". In the house was Pat, her good friend Mavis, Mr Price, and the vicar and his wife. Nelly opened her cards and placed them on the mantel. Richard and Nelly did not speak to each other during the evening. Pat was the only one that noticed, so when the parlour games had finished and everyone left, she questioned her son.

He did not give much detail but explained that he thought Nelly might have felt something for him more than just a friend.

"Maybe she just needs time," Pat said. "She's made a lot of progress over these past six months but she still struggles with things. And maybe she did see De Ville. You know she sees a lot of things we can't."

"It felt like a sign, that's all," Richard thought for a moment. "I thought I saw someone there funnily enough but I was just seeing things of course."

"Are you sure that doctor chap is dead?" Pat began washing up the glasses and threw Richard a tea towel.

"Certainly!" Richard almost chuckled at the consideration. "That's who they think Nelly killed."

"That annoys me," Pat's nose crinkled. "She wouldn't hurt a fly."

When Richard went to bed, he heard Nelly crying in her room. He knocked and let himself in. She was brushing her hair, while sobbing quietly. He didn't want to ask what was wrong. He knew she wouldn't want to tell him. Instead, he climbed on the bed and sat behind her, holding her in his arms.

"I still have nightmares," she blubbered.

"I know," he replied resting his head against hers.

"Everyone was so nice to me," she looked up at him.

"Because people care for you," Richard held her tighter. "I care about you."

She was still looking up at him and as he said his words she kissed him on the lips ever so lightly. "Thank you Richard. I care about you too."

Richard left her after tucking her in and closed the door behind him. He had not reacted to her kiss. He walked across the hallway and into his own bedroom. He shut the door behind him. He smiled before dreaming in his sleep. Nelly did the same.

Chapter Sixteen: December 1958 – Christmas Do

Nelly stared in the wall mirror at the new dress she had just put on. It was blue. Pat knocked lightly on the bedroom door and let herself in. "Oh Nelly dear, you look lovely," she smiled. "I told you it would suit you. Shall I do your hair now?"

Nelly smoothed an end of it. She looked worried. "There is nothing you can do about the colour?"

"The colour, my darling, is beautiful." Pat hugged her. "And I know Richard will adore it." She made Nelly smile.

While they were upstairs, Richard was in the kitchen trying to straighten is tie by looking at his reflection in a spoon. For some reason he felt nervous going to the Christmas party.

Finally, the ladies of the house greeted him and he had prepared a drink for them. His eyes widened when he saw Nelly. She was wearing make-up and her hair looked soft and pretty. The room had been decorated with the typical Christmas decorations. There was a Christmas tree by the fire and some holly and ivy draped over the mantel. A little piece of mistletoe was also hanging in front of it. Richard offered his arm first to Nelly and she nervously accepted. His mother instantly took his other arm and demanded to go. They walked down the lane with a skip in their stride, passing all the front doors with Christmas wreaths hanging from the door knickers. They were careful not to slip on black ice. They reached the church hall.

There were a few drunks already outside cheering happily and wishing them a merry Christmas. When they entered, the vicar took a picture of them and whisked Pat off onto the dance floor. “Fancy a drink then?” Richard asked giving Nelly a concerning shake.

“That sounds good to me!” They strolled over to the table and poured some punch into some glasses. “Is it real *drink* Rick?” Nelly sounded nervous.

He gave it a sniff and replied, “Smells like rum to me. Don’t worry I’ll look after you if you get a little tiddly.” He gave her a cheeky wink and slurped some of the punch up. In about two gulps he finished his drink and plonked the glass on the table. “Come on then!”

He gave her a tug and she swallowed the drink in one, squinting at the strong taste. Richard laughed. He took her to the dance floor and carefully put one hand on her back like she was a piece of porcelain. “Where do I put my hands?” she queried breathlessly. Her hands were trembling.

“Well, one can be put on my shoulder like this, and the other one can fit with my hand, like so.” He started swaying with the music, but she stopped him.

“But what about my feet?”

"Do you trust me?"

"Of course."

"Then let me guide you and listen to the music." He took a step forward and she followed him with a step back. So slowly but surely they were dancing. Rick and Nelly were dancing. Pat noticed them and pointed it out to her latest dance partner, the greengrocer. They watched the young couple work out their awkward first steps before becoming something more than just Doctor and Patient.

The night moved on and from a drink to the dance floor was the theme for Richard and Nelly. A slow song began and Richard had been talking to his friends from school. He had left Nelly with Pat for a while, but with the slow song playing he made his way to her and asked to dance with her again.

"Go on Nelly, I'll be fine here," said Pat, who had noticed Nelly's hesitation. She gave her a friendly nudge.

Richard took her in his arms but this time slower and a little tighter. She even clung onto his shoulder a little closer to his neck and she moved her head closer to his. They went around in a slow circle and Nelly shut her eyes for a moment.

"Rick," she whispered.

"Yes," he whispered back moving his cheek a whisker away from hers.

"I like dancing with you."

She felt him smile and he breathed a chuckle, "Me too."

Suddenly there was tap on their shoulders and a familiar voice spoke. "May I cut in?" they both looked up simultaneously and saw Nurse Chloe Caddy standing before them. Nelly immediately observed how much glamorous she was compared to her. She had redder lips and thicker eye mascara on. Her hair was a beautiful glossy auburn.

"Chloe!" Richard gasped. Nelly felt his hold on her loosen. She had lost him.

"Ricky," she whined and gave him a kiss on his cheek, leaving a smudge like marking territory. "You don't mind do you 2.5.7?"

Nelly had not been called that for a long while and was almost taken aback by her knowledge of its sensitivity. She walked away and the couple danced.

Pat rushed to her with two glasses full of punch, who had been keeping an eye on the all night, asked who the woman was.

When Nelly revealed who she was, there was a defeated tone within the voice that Pat was hurt by. She put one arm round her motherly and kissed her on top of her head. "Drink up my darling. I know there are a few fellas who would like to dance with you." She brought her to a small gathering around the table with the drink and Nelly conversed with many, even dancing with a few. But she still glanced over at Richard, who had forgotten about her completely.

Eventually, she joined Pat and a couple of the other women from the WI around a table.

“Pat,” she spoke with a decision made.

“Yes my darling girl,” Pat smiled in a loving way.

“I am very tired. May I-”

“Of course sweet-pea,” Pat interrupted. “Do you have your key?” she shook her head. “Have mine and I know Richard has his so just leave the latch when you get in.” She paused like she was considering her next move. “Shall I come with you?”

“Oh no don’t be silly! I am just not used to this.”

“I understand. I’ll check on you when I get back alright?”

“Alright.” Nelly stood up to go but felt Pat grab her arm. When she looked down Pat had puckered her lips so Nelly returned to the seat and Pat gave her a kiss on her head for a good night’s sleep.

When Nelly reached the open air, she felt the alcohol mask swirl round her like a twister. She took a deep breath and continued up the lane. A stumble here and there she believed she was doing quite well but a sudden cold spell ran down her spine like an evil shadow. She had stopped walking and stood still in the middle of the lane.

"Nelly, are you alright?" asked a male's voice. It was the greengrocer with his wife. Nelly looked up at them but she was scared of what she saw.

She screamed!

"What is it?" he asked.

She did not see his face as it was but as what it will be. It was a gaunt ghost of a face with intruding cheeks. His eyes were sunken within his sockets of his skull and his skin was looser. She turned to his wife but she was worse. Her face was bruised and blood dripped from her scalp like she had been run over.

Nelly ran away. She ran as quickly as she could, losing her shoes as she did so.

The more people she past the more she saw. Many were aged and rotten, but some like Mrs Greengrocer were horrific.

She reached the house and with a shaking hand tried to fit the key into the lock. She heard a rustle in a neighbour's bush. She turned to check and took a deep breath to calm her nerves. It was dark and hard to see but she was sure when she recognised the face. His thin, lanky stance – she would never forget. It was Doctor De Ville! She saw him grin with his revolting yellowy teeth.

She screamed!"

One of Richard's friends had seen her while walking nearby. When he asked if she was alright, Nelly didn't take another breath. She turned around slowly with tears in her eyes. "It's James remember?" he commented. And by the sight of him screamed again.

His occupation was a coal miner and with a dirty face his skull was smashed in, with blood dripping from his broken jaw. His jaw was no longer connected to the main part of the skull and hung off his head like a gruesome necklace.

She threw up where she stood and James grabbed hold of her to stop her falling. Both he and her saw the vision which was so horrifying that James ran away. The vision had a setting of the coal mines. It was a hot day, especially down in the mines as James and the others were sweating like pigs. James was watching as one of the other miners took dynamite further down the mine. He had been drinking because there was a smell of whiskey. That man laughed and carelessly he swung the dynamite in his arms. He caught James eye. As he smiled there was a sudden dead silence; a knowing moment of when something bad was going to happen. James's friend who had been standing by him suddenly shouted to run and James saw the man with dynamite be blown into pieces and a bright light stung his eyes. His friends had flung himself on top of him.

James felt heavy and couldn't hear properly. As he looked around he saw his friends die and he couldn't help them. The mine began to collapse and a large rock fell onto his legs. The agony was unbearable.

With the shock of the knowledge he released Nelly from his hold. And ran away. Nelly fell to the ground and shook uncontrollably. She saw darkness; blurred darkness.

Within a few moments she saw blurred legs running towards her. She felt someone's arms pick her up and take her into the warmth of the house. She was freezing.

Richard took her to bed and Pat brought a hot water bottle. Like distant voices, Nelly heard Richard telling off his mother for letting her go home alone. She felt a wet flannel on her forehead and the room had gone dark. She must had fallen asleep.

Chapter Seventeen: The Hangover

Nelly's eyes fluttered open slowly the following morning. Her mouth was dry and her head was heavy. She crawled out of her bed like a tired animal, groaning with her headache. Still not standing, she reached up for the doorknob; tapping it rather than opening it like she had forgotten how to use her thumbs.

In the hallway, she heard voices from downstairs. Grabbing hold of the banister tightly, her dizziness became worse. She thought she could vomit at any moment. Taking every step like it was her last she made it to the bottom of the stairs.

"There's my little bottle of gin!" Pat chuckled. "Are you feeling a little tender this morning sweetheart?"

"Ur," she stated nodding. She didn't have the energy to say yes.

"Come and sit at the table and I'll get you some juice." Nelly came into the kitchen like a snail and saw Richard sitting at the table waiting for her. She slumped on the chair next to him, feeling Pat smooth her head as a glass of orange juice was place in front of her.

"I'm sorry." She spoke with a croaked voice.

"As long as you're alright, we don't mind," Richard said kindly.

"Where's?"

"The nurse?" Pat interrupted. "She's still sleeping on the sofa in the living room." She seemed to disapprove.

Richard ignored his mother; he wanted to know more about what Nelly had seen last night. Nelly tried to describe and Pat shivered. She hated hearing the gory details. Nelly focused on James, Richard's friend who had seen her struggling last night.

As she described his appearance, Pat joined them at the table, leaning on her elbows intensely gazing at Nelly.

"Do you think," Pat began to say. "Stop me if this is crazy. But do you think that you were seeing future death?" Richard considered it and turned to Nelly to see her thoughts. Pat went on, "the fact that everyone you saw were pale and rotting would suggest it."

"Doctor De Ville wasn't," Nelly felt a shiver down her spine as she spoke his name.

"He's already dead remember," Richard reminded her. As he took her hand to reassure her, they heard a big sigh from behind them. Nelly whipped her hand away quickly and hid them under the table.

"Ugh!" Chloe groaned as she stretched into the room. "Morning." She wrapped her arms around Richard with a skimpy night dress on.

"Good Afternoon," Pat said making Nelly giggle at her sarcasm. "So not to be rude but, how long are you staying?"

"Mother!" Richard gave her a stern look.

"Well I was only enquiring as there is not a lot of room for a guest." She held her hands in front of her as defence.

"I fully understand Mrs Pearce," Chloe replied, draping herself over Richard. "I know it's always difficult having guests especially since you have two on your plates!" she chuckled playfully, but Pat didn't join her.

She stood and rested her hands on the table. "Two?" Her tone and posture had changed. Richard knew his mother's angry face and it was forming the longer they were in the room.

He was about to stand and calm her.

"Pat," Nelly said making her way to her. She had seen her anger bubbling to the surface as well. "Can we go down to the church for a walk?" she embraced her lovingly and Pat's posture weakened. She could never resist a cwtch.

They walked out together leaving Chloe and Richard alone. Chloe explained that it had been hard to find him but needed him. She loved him and wanted to continue with their engagement. Richard's thoughts drifted to Nelly.

"Please Ricky," Chloe whined and she sat on his lap. "I wove you." She kissed him harshly, biting his lip a little. "How about I get dressed and we go for something to eat?"

"Alright then," Richard lifted her up and she squealed with excitement like a little girl. Nothing was open that day as it was Christmas Eve, so in the end they met Nelly and Pat along their walk.

Pat rolled her eyes, when she saw the bright red lipstick on her son's girlfriend's lips, she couldn't help but speak her mind, "Red lipstick in mid-afternoon? What a slut!"

Nelly burst out laughing. "You can't say that."

"I would only say that to you don't worry. Anyway she deserves it after what she called you."

"What?" Nelly thought for a couple of seconds. "2.5.7? That's nothing new."

"I didn't mean that even though that is still wrong. Nelly you know you are not a guest don't you?"

Nelly didn't answer. Although she no longer felt like a guest, it wasn't her place to call it home.

"It's your home as much as mine and Richard's. You are like a daughter to me."

"Thank you Pat."

"I think we should thank Laurel. God rest her soul. She was the one that brought you to me. She knew I needed you the same as you needed me."

They stopped walking and Nelly grabbed Pat tightly round her waste. Pat wrapped her arms around her tightly. "I love you Pat."

"I love you too Nell."

Richard and Chloe reached them. "Well this looks cosy?" Chloe commented.

"We're going home getting ready for Father Christmas, if you'd like to join us," Pat was still holding Nelly's hand. Richard couldn't help but smile at them.

"Really?" Chloe did not look impressed.

"Well its Nelly's first Christmas with us and we want to make it special don't we Richard?"

"Oh yes Mum."

The four of them reached the house and went inside. They began making mince pies for Father Christmas. There was a warm fire made in the living room and as Nelly walked passed the mantel, bumping into Richard.

"Sorry," he said smiling down at her. He set his hands on her upper arms.

"Ooh, ooh, ohh!" Pat said walking in the room from the kitchen with flour all over her. "You're under the mistletoe! Kiss kiss!"

The couple looked back at one another, both their hearts beating quicker. Richard leaned closer to her, but as they puckered their lips, Chloe pushed Richard out of the way.

"Oh I'm sorry," she said. "I didn't see you both there. Nelly bowed her head with bashfulness. "Oh mistletoe!" Chloe 'noticed' it hanging above her and Richard. She kissed him passionately. Nelly moved away and returned to the kitchen with an irritated Pat.

Everyone went to bed early that night waiting to hear the jingling bells of Father Christmas's sleigh. Chloe had remained on the sofa as the others went to their separate rooms. Richard hesitated outside Nelly's door. He wasn't going to go in, but he heard Nelly's voice call hello so he felt he had to show himself.

He leaned inside. "Hi," he said simply. "Just wanted to check you were alright before turning in."

"I'm quite excited with it being Christmas Day tomorrow."

Richard sat on the end of the bed. "I've been thinking about you and the De Ville sitings?"

"Me too." She lowered her eyes.

"I think these are just visions. They're not real."

"I know. Like my nightmares."

"Exactly." Richard nodded with reassurance.

"Are you pleased Nurse Caddy is back?"

"Chloe? Yes, I suppose so. Hmm."

"You love her very much. You're going to marry her.'

"Um yes."

"I'm happy for you Richard." Nelly pulled at her duvet so it was over her fully and began to lie down. She had finished what she was going to say so Richard replied with a good night and left her alone.

If he had turned back he would have seen the tear run from Nelly's eye as he left, but he didn't. He was hiding his own tears.

Chapter Eighteen: Merry Christmas

Nelly woke up to banging. It was Pat banging a metal spoon against a saucepan. She met Richard in the hallway and both of them raced down the stairs pushing each other playfully. They were still wearing their pyjama's

"What the hell!" Chloe shouted holding her hands over her ears. Pat stopped as the three appeared in the doorway.

"Merry Christmas All!" she said excitedly. "I will be making a start on making dinner in an hour or so and Nelly is going to help me. I want you two to help too!"

All going into the living room, Pat had placed presents under the tree already and they gathered around it. Nelly plonked herself onto the floor in front and Pat sat on the edge of the sofa lighting a cigarette.

Richard joined Nelly on the floor, leaning on his hand just behind her. He was close to her and it wasn't unnoticed by Chloe who almost sat on Richard as she also sat on the floor.

Richard opened a present from his mum, which was a new watch. It wasn't too expensive looking but was very smart. He found another one with his name on and unwrapped it. It was a red scarf with a few awkward stitches in places.

"Do you like it?" Nelly asked a little worried about the dodgy stitching. "I made most of it but your Mum helped a lot."

"Not a lot, just a bit of guidance," Pat corrected her.

"I love it." He smiled at it sentimentally and noticed his name had been stitched on the end. "In fact I'll wear it now."

"Ricky," Chloe said. "I couldn't get you a proper present."

"Hmm." Pat interrupted.

"But once we're alone," she began and whispered in his ear.

"Anyway," Pat rolled her eyes. "Get the present in the corner. That one is from me for Nelly." Nelly was careful when opening it and revealed a bottle of perfume.

"It smells lovely," Nelly smiled and quickly gave Pat's present to her. Hers was a new hat. The one she had been eyeing up in the local shop down the hill. There was nothing else under the tree so Pat wanted to start the cooking, but Richard stopped her. He pulled out a little box from his trouser pocket.

"Oh Ricky," Chloe whined lovingly.

He passed it to Nelly, who was surprised at being given another present. It was a locket necklace – made of gold.

"Shall I help you put it on?" Richard smiled and Nelly just nodded with response. She thought it was beautiful, but couldn't think of the words to reply. They stood and Richard put his arms over her head and fixed it from behind her. He liked the smell of her new perfume.

After a few hours of cooking, Pat told Nelly it was time to go and get Mr Price who was also invited to Christmas dinner, since he lived alone. The air was crisp and it looked like it could rain. When Nelly knocked on the door, Mr Price's dog barked until the door was opened.

Nelly grabbed the lead and collar from the side table and put it on the dog. Mr Price already had his hat and coat on. "I'll take him for a walk before I go back, just to calm him a little," Nelly advised and took a wander up the hill.

Nelly felt the breeze touch her like small blunt needles. By the time she reached top of the hill, reaching the field, it began to sprinkle with rain. Suddenly, the little dog rushed off after seeing a squirrel and Nelly lost her grip of the lead! She needed to catch him before she returned to the house.

The small clock in the living room chimed. It had been half an hour since Mr Price had arrived. Nelly should have been back by now. Richard had noticed. He was getting worried. Chloe continued to sit basically on top of him even though he tried to push her away on a number of occasions.

"Mum, Nelly still isn't back?" he commented walking into the kitchen.

"That's strange," she stopped stirring the gravy for a moment. "She does like to wander mind but it might be best if you go get her. She'll be-"

"-at the top of the hill, I know." He finished his mother's sentence. Chloe didn't want him to go however, she tried to make him stay but he was having none of it. It was pouring with rain now.

As he placed his coat on, Pat called him. "While you find her, think about why you are out on the pouring rain, looking for her."

"I have an obligation to-"

"No Richard. Not as a doctor. Think about it." She put something in his pocket and kissed him on his head. He thought about what his mother had said as he held his hat on his head so not to lose it in the wind.

He had always seen Nelly as Patient 2.5.7 even though it was him who had refused to call her that. She had grown into a beautiful woman, who was caring and generous. He was wearing the scarf she had made for him.

There was a time that he ignored his deepest thoughts and feelings as he felt it was not being responsible. He was her doctor after all. But he wasn't anymore, not really. He hadn't been since he helped her escape the police.

Then he saw her. She was perched under a tree, sheltering from the rain. She was holding the dog in her arms.

"Nelly," he called, running towards her. She got up and smiled.

"I lost the dog and then it poured down. I was hoping it would ease."

"Nell, I want to tell you something." Richard came closer to her and she placed the dog back on his feet onto the ground. "I like you a lot."

"I know." She didn't understand what he was trying to say.

"I mean, I think about you all the time and I care about you."

"And I care for you too."

"Listen, what I'm trying to say is that I want to kiss you, I want to be with you."

"I – I don't understand. You are going to be married to Chloe?"

"I never proposed to her. She just assumed and I can't feel the same way I do for you." He reached in his pocket and found what his mother had placed inside. He hovered the mistletoe over both him and Nelly. “I love you Nell.”

Nelly leaned towards him and rested her hands on him, before she finally felt his lips against hers. Richard put his arms round her and kissed her romantically. The rain continued to pour down over them, but they didn’t care. As they continued to kiss each other, Richard placed his hat on her head so she wouldn’t get as wet.

For the first time, Nelly felt no one else around them. It was just her and Richard, plus the dog but there was no one else nudging and talking to her. She was finally at peace.

And as they stopped canoodling, Nelly replied to Richard, “I love you too.”

Chapter Nineteen: Only One Kiss

Richard pushed his hat up that was sitting on Nelly's head so she could see. He gestured for them to walk down the hill. Hand in hand they strolled not caring about the rain. The dog ran a little ahead of them, still attached to his lead. They came to the bend of the road, which is just where their house was.

Nelly faltered a moment. Richard gave her a tug not sensing it. Finally he saw the police car outside the house. Both stopped and Richard felt Nelly squeeze his hand tighter.

Pat came out with the detective shouting. They couldn't quite hear what she was saying but was pulling at the detective's arm as if to stop him from looking for them. Another policeman had seen them and was running up the road to seize her.

He grabbed hold of her brutally and hauled her to the car. She didn't resist.

"No!" Richard shouted. "Please there is no need to treat her like that!"

"Richard do something!" Pat cried. She had tears running down her cheeks as she tried to loosen the grip of the hold the police officer had on Nelly. Richard held his mother close to him. They were both crying.

"You are lucky I'm not arresting you and your son for perverting the course of justice!" the detective said while getting in the car with Nelly. They drove away. Chloe joined them outside with an umbrella and Mr Price hovered in the doorway with his dog. There were a number of people looking through their windows nearby as well.

"I don't understand," Richard said, still embracing his mother. "How did they find us?"

Pat turned to Chloe who was hiding a smile. Richard walked passed her avoiding her eye. He knew it had been her too. As everyone followed him in, he had picked up the phone.

"Ricky?" Chloe said trying to touch him. "Where are you going?"

"I'm going to borrow the farm truck and going after her." Richard spoke on the phone with the farmer and agreed to take it. He was leaving straight away.

"But Rick, what about us?"

"There is no us Chloe. There never really was."

Richard left. He didn't turn back even though he heard Chloe's cries after him. He was going to Nelly's side. He wasn't going to desert her; not now. They only shared one kiss.

Chapter Twenty: 1958-1959 – The Investigation

I

Richard wasn't allowed to visit Nelly. She had been placed in a secure unit in an asylum, until it came to court proceedings. He waited for the detective to appear from the police station to catch him alone.

But the detective didn't want to divulge any information.

"Please you must listen to me," Richard ran in front of him as the detective reached his car. He was scruffy and had not shaved or slept. "You know I was there during the fire and the doctor was alive when we left him."

"Listen Doctor Pearce, I have another witness who states that you had left Patient 2.5.7 in the building and ran back for her." The detective moved away from him.

"Who told you that?" Richard was becoming more frustrated the more he thought about it.

"So it's true?"

"Was it Chloe Caddy?"

"I can't give you that information. It would be better for you just to let things lie. I've seen the patient's file. I know her history." he turned to the car to unlock the door.

"Wait?" Richard rubbed his head. "Everything burnt in the fire? How could you possibly find her file?"

He saw the detective think about the logistics of his argument. He agreed with him. “You said in your statement that you saw someone else within the fire?”

“Yes, Matron.” The detective had a spurt of energy and got into his car. “I’m coming with you!” Richard sprinted to the passenger seat and got in.

“You can’t. This is a police matter.”

“I can be useful. Please?”

The detective started the engine and drove quickly to Matron’s house. Richard noticed the curtains twitch as they pulled up in the driveway. The house was dark with a minimal garden. When they came to the entrance, the door opened without them knocking.

Richard hadn’t seen matron since the fire. She looked older. It might had been something to do with the fact she was wearing her own clothes and not the uniform he had always seen her in.

She let them inside and the décor had not been updated since the 1940s judge by the blackouts and the taped crosses on the windows.

“I had a feeling you might come Doctor Pearce,” she said taking a seat in the arm chair. “You were always such an inquisitive man.”

“Tell me about the file Matron,” Richard took a seat, almost forgetting the detective was with him.

"I saved the file from the fire. I needed to." She seemed nervous. It reminded him of when she was frightened by 2.5.7.

The detective interrupted the conversation. He had not sat down, but hovered in the room like a fly. "You live alone don't you?" he had confirmed this last time he was there, Richard could tell.

"You know I do. I've never married."

"Hmm."

"Why do you ask detective?" Richard questioned his motive. He couldn't see what the detective was trying to do.

"Oh it's just there was a man's coat on the coat stand when we came in. We're still wearing ours, Matron, I presume you wouldn't wear it."

"Oh urr urr," Matron was faltering. "It was my fathers. He died."

"I see." The detective took a seat next to Richard. "So you saved the file regarding Patient 2.5.7. Did you save any others?"

"No." she shifted in her seat.

"Any reason?"

"I saw it and picked it up. That's about it."

"But the file was in the basement at the time of the fire? I remember." Richard sat up a little as he spoke. He saw Matron was beginning to sweat.

"I was wandering around within the building for a while same as you. There is nothing more I can say."

"Thank you for your cooperation," the detective nudged Richard to leave so he followed.

"Where are we going now?" Richard asked as he got into the car.

"To see the remains again." There was a squeal of the wheels as they drove off the gravelly driveway. Time seemed to move quickly for Richard as if felt like moments before they arrived.

As it had been so long since fire, there was not much left of the body, but they still had the items that were found. There was the ID badge, scuffed around the edges but was clearly Doctor De Ville's. There had been photos taken of the body when it was found and Richard studied them. He explained that judging by the shot wound it looked like the victim had been shot after burning in the fire.

There was also some remains of a white coat that read *Doctor* and what looked like a beginning on a *D.* But Richard noticed something. "Wait this has coffee stains on it," Richard commented.

"Your point?" the detective couldn't grasp his revelation.

"Doctor De Ville never drank coffee?" The two men looked at each other a moment like they were thinking the same thing.

"I think I need to visit the Matron again." The detective went back to his car. Richard didn't go with him this time. He had agreed to meet his mother at the old asylum grounds. They had bid each other a goodbye but they knew they were going to meet again to give each other the information they may have gathered.

II

Meanwhile, Pat was sitting on an uncomfortable wooden chair. She wiggled on it to try and get a little comfortable, holding her bag on her lap. It had been almost an hour to wait. She wasn't a very patient woman at the best of times but was on her best behaviour due to the circumstances. She needed a cigarette, but one of the nurses had already told her off for smoking as it panicked certain patients. She ruffled her back hair to tidy herself.

Eventually a nurse approached her and with a smile and a kind manner, took her to a door. "Please be careful not to excite her," the nurse seemed nice. Pat liked her.

"I've brought soup for her. Is that alright? They have checked it." Pat lifted her handbag as a gesture.

"There'll be a small opening that you can push it through." The nurse unlocked the door and let Pat go into the room first. It was grey with one chair facing a glass wall. "The opening is just there Mrs Pearce," she gestured at the glass wall along the floor. The nurse was right, there was a small flap. Pat thought it odd and when she turned around to the nurse she had already left.

She took out the Tupperware box filled with cold soup from her bag. She didn't realise Nelly was already there.

When the nurse returned with a thought, Pat caught her before she rushed out again. "I just wanted to warn you that she may not speak," the nurse said with an essence of worry in her voice. "She hasn't said much since she scared one of the nurses."

"Excuse me nurse," Pat replied. "Where is she?" The nurse had a sympathetic expression and pointed to the corner of the room on the other side of the glass wall. And Pat saw her. Laying in the corner, was Nelly curled up in the foetal position facing the wall. Her room was padded from top to bottom.

Pat knocked on the wall but Nelly didn't budge. She called her name and knocked again. This time Nelly rolled over so she was facing the glass wall. When she sat up, she recognised Pat who was still holding her fist in a knocking fashion. Nelly could only crawl closer to her; her straight jacket was too tight to do anything else.

"I brought you some soup. It's cold mind." Pat pushed the Tupperware box through the hole in the wall and Nelly struggled to drink from it. She drank like a dog. "Richard is going to get you out of here."

Nelly just nodded and continued to drink. Her eyes had deep blackened bags under them and her hair had been chopped short, in some sort of uneven bob style.

"Are you alright?" Pat couldn't think of what else to say.

"They are giving me sedatives," she croaked. "I'm sorry to be so dull."

"I like your hair," Pat tried to get her talking. Her state reminded her of when she first met her. Weak; frightened; lonely; innocent.

"They cut it so I wouldn't hurt myself. That's why I'm wearing this." Nelly looked down at the strait jacket.

"Don't you worry my darling. We'll get you out don't worry." She placed her hand onto then glass and Nelly rested her head on the other side. The nurse came back and escorted Nelly's mother out of the room. Nelly returned to her corner and cried alone in her padded cell.

When Pat and the nurse reached the reception again, Pat noticed the nurse linger as she was putting her coat on. "Nurse," Pat turned to her. "When you said one of the nurses was scared by her?"

"That was me," the nurse confessed. "She knew things that only a few people knew. It freaked me out if I'm honest." She blurted.

"What did she say?" Pat sat on one of the uncomfortable wooden seats.

"I took her to her room, which was a normal one with a bed and some minimal furniture." The nurse hesitated but continued. "The first night I heard her crying so I went in to try and comfort her. She told me she wasn't crying because of that. Then she did the strangest thing."

"What?"

"She tapped her foot against the metal of the bed. It was the same rhythm that I had heard in that same room."

"I don't understand."

"You see the last person in the room... hung themselves. The banging was the same as that patients feet knocking against the wall." She had tears in her eyes. "I remember when I heard that noise, I knew there was something wrong and then, when I entered, I saw her hanging-" She through her head to her knees and whimpered. Pat patted her back.

"It wasn't your fault," Pat struggled with words.

"But when Nelly or Patient 2.5.7 as they are calling her, turned to me while lying in the bed and asked if she could swap rooms because she couldn't stand the sight of the patient hanging from the ceiling, I felt sick. I didn't know how to react."

"Of course you didn't," Pat continued to rub the nurse's back as she spoke. "Nelly is special. She can see things that we can't. That doesn't mean she deserves to be in here."

The nurse nodded and watched as Pat left in a cab. When she had lost sight of her, she went back to see Nelly in the padded room. The nurse went inside and found her crying. Nelly looked up at her and flinched as she moved closer. The nurse assured her she wasn't going to hurt her and she loosened the strait jacket.

She didn't say anything else. She left Nelly alone. She curled up into her corner again. She had stopped crying though.

III

Richard met with his mother at the old Gravehill site. It had been over a two years since the fire, yet there had been nothing done with it. The pile of rubble had been scavenged during the years so there was nothing to see, but Richard felt a certain solace at being there. It reminded him of the times he had spent with his patient. How he had begun to fall in love with her the moment he saw her discoloured eyes and her ever so light hair.

The grounds had been untouched. Pat had walked around it already as she had been waiting a while for Richard to turn up. When he caught up to her, they continued to stroll around as Richard told the events inside the building that was once standing.

All of a sudden they heard a hiss amongst the trees. Richard held his mother behind him as he moved closer. The hiss sound was heard again.

"Who's there?" Richard called. And out from behind a tree came Matron. She was wearing an overcoat as well as sunglasses that she didn't need.

"I thought I would find you here," she said with a whisper.

Pat caught up with them, who had held back waiting to see the person first. "Why are you here?" Richard asked.

"I couldn't speak at home," she hesitated. "But I want to give you this." She revealed a folder from within her jacket. "It should help explain things for you."

Richard opened it immediately and it was a photograph of a young Doctor De Ville and a small child. It was a girl. On the back it read 'Daddy and Chloe'.

"You don't think?" Pat muttered, but Richard had already began to run. She turned to Matron who was still standing with her. "Is it really Chloe Caddy?"

"Yes," Matron confirmed. "And he wasn't happy when she failed him."

"How did she fail?"

"She was meant to find out where Patient 2.5.7 was, but she told the police out of jealousy."

"Wait?" Pat gripped Matron's arms tightly. "He's alive?"

"I thought you realised that? That's why I came here to warn you. He's set to kill Patient 2.5.7 for what she knows." She also explained that he had been staying with her in hiding.

"WHAT?" Pat grabbed her chest with shock. "What does she know that is so terrible?"

"That Doctor De Ville tortured and killed patients in the asylum and that the man Patient 2.5.7 was condemned to the asylum for was murdered by Doctor De Ville. Doctor De Ville killed him out in the open because he escaped. Patient 2.5.7 found him."

"The man took her to his body so someone could reveal what he was doing." Pat almost felt proud at what Nelly had been holding all this time. "Where is he now?"

Matron bit her lip. "I think he's on his way to finish the job."

Pat knew what she needed to do. She ran.

IV

Richard reached the old steps he vaguely remembered as home. He ran up the flights of stairs skipping a step as he went. He bashed the door in, creating aloud echoing bang.

"Chloe!" he yelled angrily. He was panting.

"How dare you barge in here like this!" She shouted back. "You have no-"

"Shut up about rights you stupid bitch," Richard threw her onto the sofa. "You're a liar!" The room was dark as the curtains were shut. It was hard to see.

"And what are you? Leading me on all this time!" she thumped her hands onto the sofa.

"You knew how I felt long before you pushed for attention!"

"My father is a good man. He did what he needed to do to those people; if you can call them that."

"Those people have feelings and just need support. What your father did was unforgivable!" Chloe moved into the light, revealing a bruised face. "Who did that to you?" She turned away. "Wait you said 'is'?"

She began to chuckle.

"Chloe!" he seized her by the arm. He frightened her as he growled.

"You should have kept your promise to her." Her voice shook.

"What?"

"You promised to always be there for her?"

"I don't follow?" Richard took a step back.

"You're not there now are you?" she smirked. Richard's eyes glazed over. She cackled again.

And he ran.

He ran as fast as he could hearing as he left, "She will always be just the mental patient, 2.5.7!!"

V

Pat pulled up outside the asylum in a cab. She threw money at the driver, running inside. She tried to run passed reception but a man stopped her. "I need to get in there! Life death situation! Please!" He shook his head at her.

He walked her back inside reception and a nurse came in to see if she could help. It was the same nurse she had met before. Pat explained that she needed to check on Nelly but the nurse pulled an apologetic face, refusing to let her go in.

"I can assure you that this is a secure facility and you've seen the sort of place she's in."

"But she's in danger. A madman is going to kill her!"

"I'm afraid I can't do anything without a doctors-"

"Get me a doctor then! But please someone needs to go and guard her or something!"

Suddenly a siren started. The nurse rushed to desk just outside the reception boundary. She looked up at Pat and before she even spoke she knew what she was going to say. "It's Nelly's room." All three, including the man of security rushed to the room. The glass wall had been smashed and a trail of blood leading from the padded room to the visitor's room. It was too late. Pat put her hands on her knees and breathed heavily. She was becoming short of breath. The nurse tried to comfort her as the man went on the search for her with others.

Pat couldn't just sit and wait; she needed to do something. She went through the hospital looking and then she saw something. Walking to it, she found a red smudge on the corner of the wall. She had been dragged into that room. Pat looked down the hall. There was no one else around. She took a deep breath.

She took the handle and pushed it down, creating an eerie creak. Pulling it open, there were stairs leading upwards. "God that's a lot of stairs," she moaned under her breath. She started to walk up them. They got steeper the further she went.

She heard a noise behind her.

She stopped; listening.

Nothing so she continued.

She heard it again.

She halted for a second time and suddenly someone grasped her shoulder. She screamed. Richard put his hand over her mouth to stop her screaming.

"It's me Mum, me!" as he released his hold of her she sighed with relief before hitting him a few times.

"Stupid boy!" she hissed. "You frightened me!"

Richard opened his mouth to speak but they heard another noise at the top of the stairs. He gestured with a bob of his head to keep going.

Reaching another door, it was still partially open and they felt a breeze coming from it. It led to the roof. Carefully step-toeing so not to make too much noise, they walked along the wall with their backs against it. Pat tried to quieten her wheeze.

Finally they saw him. His thin, tall figure with his greasy hair blowing in the wind. Laying on the floor, Nelly's leg was bleeding. He had sliced it. She was still restrained in a strait jacket, she was defenceless.

"Nelly," Pat uttered uncontrollably.

De Ville turned with a snarl. There was madness in his eyes.

"Let her go De Ville," Richard declared.

"Ha," De Ville cackled. "Why should I? She's my patient isn't she?"

"Not any more, she's not!" De Ville pulled out a knife as Richard moved closer. He laughed again as he saw Richard's fear within his eyes. Nelly groaned as she woke. She was woozy from the loss of blood. Richard heard the door creak from where they came. "Why did you do it then De Ville? Why did you kill all those people?"

"People? They weren't people," he sneered. "Patients at best. Monsters. Like her." He pointed the knife at Nelly. "She doesn't understand knowledge and strength. She's weak like the lot of them. I was only showing them their potential."

"You call torturing people potential?" Richard moved a little closer and saw in the corner of his eye, the detective with other policemen had joined them on the roof.

"I was surprised really on how much pain some of them could take. Like the last one. He took the thumb screw like it was just a walk in the park. And that's what he did." He laughed again. "He escaped and went to a park. And who do I meet but a little insane girl who sees dead people, soon to be known as my next patient – 2.5.7."

"Don't call her that!" Pat interrupted.

"And who are you?!"

"Someone who cares for that poor girl!"

"Mum shut up please!" Richard whispered to her and pushed her back behind him.

"You care for the likes of a girl who spends most of her time trying to decide if you're real or not. She's barely human herself."

"I am human," Nelly sat up, wiggling out of the strait jacket that had become loose. "And that woman and doctor over there have shown me how to be human, unlike you, who just made me frightened of my own shadow!" She managed to stand on one leg, pushing herself up. "You killed those people because you wanted to not because you felt they were better off. You pushed and prodded me because you wanted to see me and the others suffer out of power and out of greed!"

"You little Fucker!" he shouted and threw himself at her with the knife still in his hand. Richard echoed her screams as he fought for the knife. Punching and biting, they scuffled. The police moved in. De Ville created the upper hand and was pushing down on the knife as Richard was underneath him, trying to avoid the sharp edge. De Ville managed to scratch Richard's face, but with the police shouting to put down the weapon, Nelly shoved De Ville off the man she loved. He lost his grip of the knife that had fallen near Pat, who had kicked it away.

Nelly clutched De Ville's head and place her forehead against his. "You think I'm crazy?" she cried. "Have a see at what I live with every day! And always remember those numbers of 2.5.7!"

Suddenly a bright light flashed between them and De Ville's screams pierced everyone's ears. For De Ville, he felt all the pain that Nelly had felt during their 'sessions' or 'consultations'. The thumb screws, the electrotherapy, the stretchings, the stabbings and not to forget the sewing skins. Finally, with all that pain pulsating through his body, she showed him the darkness. The place where all badly treated souls went when they died at his hand. They had been waiting for this moment for a long time. And finally his mind was trapped there forever.

As she released him, her energy had gone and she fell to the floor. De Ville was still screaming. The police took him away while he was still screaming. They say De Ville died still screaming. Richard never asked what Nelly had shown him. He didn't dare to. He held her in his arms as they watched the police take De Ville away. Pat joined them. Patient 2.5.7 was finally free.

Chapter Twenty One: The release

Nelly stretched while in her hospital bed. She shuffled up and realised a few people were waiting for her to wake. She struggled to her feet as her leg was still a bit sore. There were a number of nurses and her doctor with the detective. He nodded in acknowledgement.

They took her out of the room, giving her a bag with some clothes and little money.

"You are free," the detective said. "Doctor Pearce is coming to collect you."

"I'm free?" she stuttered. "I can leave?"

"Yes," replied her doctor. "You are discharged."

"And I don't need to go back to the asylum?"

"No."

Once she had put on the clothes from the bag she was taken to the main entrance and the doors were opened for her.

"Do you not want to wait for Doctor Pearce?" the detective asked.

"Could you give him this note please? Pat already knows but I thought I'd better write it down for him." She passed him a crumpled note.

She stepped outside and felt the breeze touch her skin like an old friend. As it blew her hair out of her face, she walked. She walked away from her past. She walked away from her fears. She was gone.

Richard drove up in a cab outside the hospital. He grabbed the small bouquet of flowers on the seat next to him and ran inside. With a grin on his face, he asked for Nelly but saw the nurse's disheartened expression as she advised she will get the doctor.

Nelly's doctor, whom Richard never knew the name of, came into reception with a firm handshake. "Ah Doctor Pearce," he spoke with a steady voice.

"Sorry I'm a little late, I wanted to get her something," Richard gestured to the flowers.

"I'm sorry Doctor Pearce, but she has left already."

"What do you mean?" Richard lowered the flowers.

"She gave the detective a note for you, but she was discharged about an hour ago."

"I see."

"The detective is in the canteen if you would like to see him."

"I'm here," the detective came through the door into the reception. He handed Richard the crumpled note. With a tremble Richard grasped it in his hand and left the hospital without saying another word. Still holding the flowers he opened the note:

Thank you Richard. I need to find my own way in this world but you will always be in my heart. Love Nelly.

"Are you alright Doctor Pearce?" the detective asked. Richard dropped the flowers and turned to go out the door. He never returned.

Chapter Twenty Two: 2014 – An Old Doctor's Story

Kirsty had ignored Joe's advice and returned the next day to Richard's room. He had told her about the full investigation with Patient 2.5.7. She thought it sad that the patient left him without saying goodbye.

She entered the building a little later than usual. She was quite excited as she wanted to know if Richard ever saw the patient again. She wished the nurse at reception a good morning and strolled up the stairs casually. At the top of the stars she caught sight of another nurse, who smiled and came over. She gave her the pills Richard needed to take and since she was heading that way, she thought it might be easier for her to give them to him.

In a small cup, were two small tablets. She walked down the corridor and noticed something strange. Richard's door was ajar. She had hesitated and peered down either end of the corridor. It was quite dark with the patterned wallpaper. She peeped through the open door and she heard a scuffle.

Barging in she saw Joe holding a pillow over Richard's face, which was struggling on the bed.

"HELP!" she screamed and Joe swivelled round. His mad expression frightened Kirsty, who began to back away as he moved closer to her.

"You shouldn't have done that," he hissed. He cracked his hands.

Richard was choking to breathe after almost suffocating, but he grabbed the lamp on the side table and threw it with all his might, hitting Joe on the back of the head. By this time, others had rushed in and pinned him down. They held his arms behind his back and he spat in Richard's direction.

"Who are you?" the old man croaked as Kirsty helped him up.

"You killed my mother!"

"What?"

"The way you described her in your story, 'Nurse Chloe Caddy'; she and my grandfather were trying to make the world a better place!"

"You're Chloe's boy?"

"I promised my mother on her death bed that I would hunt you down and kill you and your slut of a patient!" The police started pulling him away.

"Wait a minute," Richard called. "I loved your mother but she was selfish and didn't care about anyone else but herself. And don't you ever call her patient again!"

The police took him away, leaving Kirsty alone with Richard. He took a seat by the window and watched as the police car drove away.

"Did you ever see Chloe again?" Kirsty asked.

"God no," Richard shook his head. "She was just as bad as her father. She had no respect for the patients. I should have seen that earlier, but I was taken over by lust for her. It was nothing more."

"What about Nelly?" Kirsty sounded hopeful.

"Ha," he chuckled lightly. "I did see her again, yes. Came across her. Strange really. It was a few years later but when I saw her, it was like I had never left her side."

Chapter Twenty Three: 1963 – A Few Years Later

Richard slept on the train, but as it jolted to a stop, he jumped up and looked around. One of his colleagues smiled at him. He pointed at his watch and then to the sign on the station. Richard acknowledged they were one stop away from reaching their seminar. Richard had aged a little, revealing a little grey on his side burns.

Within the cabin, there was a couple with them, overly connected to each other. Even when the man stood up to grab the lady's bag from above in the luggage compartment, their hands still clung together like they could not survive without the other.

Richard turned away back out the window and watched as the scenery flashed by like a smeared picture. Eventually he felt the train slowing until a similar jolt brought the train to a stop. The couple jumped up first and with an irritating lover's giggle they rushed out of the carriage. Richard gestured for his colleague to get off first, which he did with a shrug of his hat.

The platform was busy. The whole of London was busy. Richard quickened his pace as he tried to keep up with his colleague and as he pushed through the crowd to reach the pavement, he saw his colleague holding a black cab. He gave him a wave.

Both sitting in the cab, the cabby asked "where to?" and his colleague advised with a toss of his hand. They were going to The Queen Hotel.

"I hate conferences," Richard's colleague stated.

"At least you won't have to make a speech about the *skin decay and its effects on investigations*," Richard moaned.

"You'll be fine."

"John, there are about 200 of us in this conference. And they all probably know a lot more than me."

John sniggered.

The cab pulled up outside the hotel. It looked quite posh and the reception was large and pristine. They checked in and went straight to their twin bedroom. John dumped his luggage onto his choice of bed, then throwing himself onto it. He placed his hands behind his head and shut his eyes for a few moments.

Richard put his case on the dresser and checked his wallet. He had enough money for dinner this evening without having to go to the bank.

"It's almost time to go down there mate," John commented looking at his watch. It was 10.20am.

Richard grunted in response. He checked his tie and said, "I'll have a breath of fresh air first I think. Meet you in there?"

“Righteo.” John stood up and patted him on the back as he left. Richard checked his pockets and took the lift to reception. As he walked through reception, then out the building, he lit a cigarette. It relaxed him. The road was busy and there was a smog in the air of the exhausts. He glanced in the window and saw people going into the conference room. He thought about what he was going to say when it was his turn.

“Doctor Pearce? Is that you?” a man’s voice asked.

Richard looked up and saw a man that he hadn’t seen in about a year. “Detective?” he replied. The detective smiled and nodded.

“Call me Frank,” he said. This was the first time Richard ever heard his name. During the investigations relating to Gravehill, he had never taken notice of him.

“How are you?” Richard asked politely.

They shook hands and Frank smiled again. Richard just grunted in response. There wasn’t really a lot to say.

“Good, it’s nice to see you. Are you visiting?”

“I’ve got a conference,” he commented, pointing at the hotel behind him.

“I heard you were working in forensics these days.”

“Well it’s thanks to you for giving me a recommendation.” Frank had noticed Richard’s precision while investigating with him and had a word with one of the friends in forensics to give Richard a chance. They had even worked together on a couple of cases.

"Part of me thought you were visiting Eleanor, when I saw you. I'm working here now."

Richard had not been listening closely enough. He thought he had misheard. "When did you transfer?" he asked taking his final puff of his cigarette.

"Three months ago or there about. Eleanor looks good mind, you seen her?"

"What?" Richard focused back on the detective.

"Nelly?" Frank raised his eyebrows with a concerning nod.

"You've seen her? Where?"

"Well, she works around here. I always bump into her in the café down the road."

"You mean she lives here!?"

Before Frank could answer, Richard rushed down the busy street and found the café on the corner. He bolted inside and halted at the back of the queue. There was no one he recognised there. No one that even looked like her. He took his wallet out of his jacket pocket and pulled out a crumpled photograph of him and her. He rubbed his thumb over it sentimentally. It had been from Christmas 1958.

Finally he heard the typical words, "What can I get you?" When he looked up he saw a pretty woman standing behind the counter.

"Um, yes," he croaked. "Have you seen this woman?" He showed her the picture. At first her mouth twisted to the left in thought.

"Ah yeah except her hair is different. It's definitely Ellie."

"Ellie?" Richard couldn't hide his pleasure. "Do you know where she is? I need to see her."

He could tell the waitress was nervous to tell him initially but soon she explained she was at work at an office two streets away. She came in every day to get a hot chocolate. The waitress scribbled the address on a napkin. After thanking her, he strolled out of the café with caution. He walked mindlessly through the crowds until he felt a strong hand grip his arm. He looked up. It was john. He dragged him back to the hotel frantically.

"You're on next!" he hissed as they sneaked into the large room filled with doctors. They sat at the back and the older gentleman that was stood in front of the microphone introduced him. John shoved him.

Richard stood up and walked from the back of the room to the front with the echoing of his footsteps. He still had

the napkin in his hands. He shook the older man's hand as he reached the stage and stood in from of the microphone.

He coughed, pulling out his notes from his chest pocket.

He began but cut himself off. He was lost within the napkin. His thoughts had drifted to the patient. He heard distant coughs from the audience and a faint comment asking if he was alright, but he did not respond. He stared at the napkin as if it wasn't even real. The waitress's writing was curvy and close together, and the harder he stared the more he saw the three numbers – 2.5.7.

Finally he felt someone touch his shoulder. It was the older gentleman. In that same moment, Richard ran out of the room, dropping his notes on the floor. He dodged the people within the reception and knocked a few people over as he did so. He ran down the road and followed the signs of street names before he noticed the building in Trafalgar Square. He strolled up to it and on entry the receptionists lifted their heads and smiled.

He cleared his thought nervously. "I was hoping you could help me," he croaked.

One of the women nodded and replied, "Of course. Do you have an appointment?"

"No. I'm looking for someone. They work here I believe."

"Alright?"

He pulled out a picture and pushed it along the table for them to see. Both of the women stood up over the counter to get a better look. "You may know her as Ellie?" He thought about the woman in the café.

"Hmm, not too sure to be honest," said one.

"Looks it a little bit like Nora actually, except her hair is all wrong," commented the other.

"Nora?"

"She's in post."

"Post?"

"Yes in the post department. I'll give her call now for you." She picked up the phone. "What's the name?"

"Richard Pearce."

As she spoke to *Nora* on the phone, Richard felt his heart beating quickly. A number of scenarios ran through his mind as he watched. One prominent idea was that she will tell the receptionist that she does not know him and he will never get to see her; another was that she would let him see her and it isn't even her in the first place.

She put the phone down.

"If you go through those double doors," she explained. "Then take the second left, down the steps you will find the post room."

“Thank you.” He did as she had said and found the staircase. It was quite dark and the stairs spiralled. As he reached the final steps he came to a door. It read: POST ROOM.

He knocked.

No answer.

He pushed the handle down and the door creaked as he opened it. The room was filled with shelves upon shelves of envelopes. “I’ll be with you in a moment,” a voice said within the stacks.

He recognised it immediately. But then he saw a brown haired lady stand from being hidden by stacks of mail. He couldn’t see her face straight away. She clamoured over some piles and he recognised her movements straight away. It was her.

And then he saw her face. It was definitely her.

“Hi,” she said with a nervous echo. She was wearing the necklace he had bought her.

“Hi Nelly.” She smiled at hearing him say her name. They didn’t touch; not even a hand shake; but he followed her as she took him deeper into the room.

“I have to keep working but we can talk while I am doing it?”

“Ok.”

They didn't talk much. He just watched her work. His eyes fixated on her like he was afraid to even blink just in case he lost her again. As she smiled he did and as she spoke he nodded. Eventually she told him that she was studying English literature in night school with her friend from the café.

He told her that he was supposed to be at a conference giving a speech about skin to many doctors, but he decided to visit her.

"What time do you finish?" Richard asked.

"In an hour or so."

"Could I buy you dinner?"

"I'd like that." Nelly smiled at him and took his hand. Before he left he kissed her on the cheek and left her to it.

When it was near the time of her finishing, Richard sat on a bench outside her work. He had flowers in his hands and he had changed his suit. It was now a dark grey, still with a sixties flare. The weather looked dull; it was probably going to rain any minute. He raised the collar of his coat a little and straightened his hat.

Nelly came out of the building and gently leaped over to him. He couldn't get used to her new look. He offered his arm and she hesitated. Not deterred, he offered again and this time she gently slipped her hand under his arm.

He felt her squeeze a little. There was almost a paused moment to see if anything would happen. It didn't.

For a while they just walked through the city, along the pavements and even passed Buckingham Palace. Finally, as it began to sprinkle with rain, Nelly suggested to go to her favourite place to eat; the chip shop.

They had a bag of chips each and Nelly grabbed his hand tugging him out of the rain. Down a few streets and they reached a door to a tall building. It was a house split into flats. It reminded him of his flat he had in Oxford just after the fire.

"We'd better get out of the rain before we eat," she said taking out a key from her bag. After thrusting the door open with a stiff shove, they walked up a flight of stairs and she opened her front door. It was a simplistic room with something like a kitchen on the side. The room consisted of a bed, some drawers and then a cooker and a refrigerator. She walked over to the window and picked up, what looked like, an old blackout board from the war.

She plonked it on the bed and sat on one side. Richard sat on the other and put the bags of chips of the blackout board. After Nelly removed the wig she had been wearing, it revealed her glossy almost white hair that Richard remembered so well. They started to eat. He was glad it had only been a wig.

“So how did your conference go after you left my work?” Nelly asked.

“Boring, but it’s done got a train booked for tomorrow though.”

“When is it?”

“11.30.”

“I’ll be in work then so I won’t be able to wave you off.”

“Do you like work?”

“It’s alright,” she paused. “There’s not many people down where I am so that’s good.”

“Do you get lonely?”

“Sometimes, but-” she stopped herself.

“But what?”

“It’s only when I think of the time we spent together.”

“I miss you Nell,”

“Me too.” They ate their chips. “I am sorry for leaving without saying goodbye.”

“I understand why you did it so I forgive you.”

They smiled.

“Do you like living in the city?” He asked moving the board off the bed.

"I prefer the village. Less people." She leaned back at the top of the bed and he followed her, wrapping his arms around her. They laid together for a long while. "What hotel are you staying in?"

"Oh um The Queen Hotel, it's nice. I suppose I'd better be getting back. I'm sharing with another doctor."

"It's too late to go out there now."

"Well, it's not proper to be in a lady's bedroom after dark."

"I think we're past that aren't we?"

He smiled and gently touched her chin to kiss her lightly on the lips. He felt her nervousness but as he held her tighter she clung to him too. He felt her hand smooth down his back and pull at his shirt so it was no longer tucked in. He had waited so long to touch her again. Part of him thought he never would.

He rubbed his hand from her thigh to her waist as she clung to the back of his neck. He pulled her closer to him as they continued to kiss each other like it was going to be their last. Nelly's dress had been loosened during the canoodling and slipped off her left shoulder. Richard smoothed his hand on her bare skin, but he felt the cloth on her arm. She flinched.

Pulling away from each other, Richard saw Nelly's concern. He tugged her dress down a little further, revealing the numbers. Nelly bit her lip nervously. She thought it might put him off her, but Richard lent over her and kissed her on her arm passionately. He climbed on top of her as he moved his kisses to her lips again. His shirt buttons were completely undone by now and he loved the light tug of his hair, Nelly started doing as her legs rubbed against his.

He paused for a moment. “Are you sure you want me to stay?” he asked, trying to conceal his desire for her.

She kissed him and replied, “I have always wanted you to stay.” She knocked her nose with his playfully and kissed him again.

He spent the night.

Chapter Twenty Four: Is This the End of the Story?

I

Richard's Morning After

Richard woke by the sunlight from the window. He stretched with his eyes still shut. When he opened them, Nelly was not lying next to him. He sat up and looked around. She had left a note.

I have left for work. Last night – I will never forget. You know goodbyes are hard for me.

He stayed sitting for a while. Then he noticed the clock. Ten to ten! He grabbed his clothes and rushed out the door. He didn't wear his coat as it was quite warm. It still looked like it was going to rain though.

When he reached the hotel, he met John in the reception. "And where have you been?!" he asked jokingly. "You dog!"

"Have you already checked out?" he didn't want to answer that question.

"No not yet was waiting for you," he pulled a key out of his pocket and chucked it towards him. "Grab your things and I'll get a cab sorted. A lot of the others have already gone."

When Richard had a quick shower and checked his room for all his ·things, his mind focused on Nelly. He remembered when he had first met her. Her mad, messy white hair and her constant distant conversations, made him smile even now. He was leaving her like he did when he sent her to that home. It was the worst decision he had ever made. He opened his wallet and pulled out his photograph of Nelly. She had grown up since then but somehow still held her innocence within.

He picked up his suitcase and left the room heading down to the reception where John was waiting for him. On sight he waved and John disappeared out of the entrance to a cab. Richard felt sad giving back his key for his room. He pushed it across the reception desk and the woman behind said, "I hope you enjoyed your stay Sir."

Her kind gesture echoed through his mind like a teasing threat. He had enjoyed his stay but it made him not want to leave. No. It made him want to take something with him.

The porter took his bag to the cab, but Richard walked straight passed him. "Sir?" Richard heard him say as he briskly strode passed.

"Richard?" John called. "Richard? Where are you going?"

Suddenly Richard stopped. He walked back to the cab and saw the confused expression on his friend's face. He didn't reply at first. He took his suitcase from the porter and nodded courteously.

"Richard! What are you doing?" John asked again. "Our train leaves in half an hour!"

Richard turned again beginning to run down the street. He called back a reply that John did not quite hear. "To take her with me!" he had said.

He shoved and pushed through the crowded streets and into the area of Nelly's work, just off Trafalgar Square. He rushed inside the building and saw the same ladies behind the tall desk. He smiled, be it a little weathered after the run. But he still managed to pant the request. "Could I see Nora please?"

The women looked at one another with concern and his smile fell. "I'm afraid she gave in her notice just this morning," advised one of the ladies.

"What?" Richard could hardly voice his shock.

"I'm afraid so," said the other lady. "It was a surprise to us all. She said she had to get away?"

Richard backed out of the building and stood for a moment. He didn't understand why she would suddenly quit her job. He decided to go to her flat in the hope to find her but when he arrived there was no answer from the bell.

He rang it again, but this time with an essence of urgency. Finally, a man answered. Richard took a step back as soon as he glimpsed him. He was a scruffy man in a vest and shorts. “Who you after?”

“Um,” Richard croaked. “The first floor flat.”

“The brunette?”

“Yes.”

“Well she’s gone mate.”

“Gone?”

“Yeah. Paid rent up for the month and scarpered.”

“That isn’t possible I was only here last-” Richard stopped himself. He didn’t want to damage any reputation.

“I know you were. You left after ‘err too. But she came back, ‘anded me the keys and took her stuff with her.”

“I can’t believe it.”

“Come in.” The man gestured for Richard to follow and took him to the same flat he had once spent a night with the woman he loved.

He went inside and the man was right. It was empty. All that was left was the black board on top of the bed. The man let him out. “Thank you for that,” Richard said solemnly.

He walked down the steps. “Listen mate,” the man said while standing in the doorway. “She said to me when she was leaving that she had to get away; and that she’s not very good at goodbyes. I don’t know whether that was for me or a message for someone else but there you have it.” The man couldn’t help but feel sorry for the guy. Richard sensed it.

As Richard nodded gratifyingly, he turned with one swift movement and walked away. He shoved one of his hands in his trouser pocket and swung his suitcase back and fore with the other. He was too late for that booked train now. And it had started to rain heavily while he had gone into the house. He pushed his hat down over his face to shade from it.

It was quite a while away from the station but he couldn’t be bothered catching a cab. He walked; passing the many busy people along the way. All the people trying to get out of the rain, but Richard didn’t care; not anymore.

When he reached the station he bought another ticket for the train. “When is the next train to Oxford?” he asked the ticket man.

“There’s been a delay since the rain I’m afraid. A tree fell on the track. We’re hoping it’ll be here by three. So another hour to wait.”

“Thank you.” Richard wasn’t really listening.

He went to platform three and decided to wait for the train to pass through before walking over to platform four. There was a metal bridge stood across platform three and four.

He leaned on the side of the staircase and watched the train pass by. It was getting colder due to the rain. He lifted his collar a little. The train chugged passed and he stared through the gaps of the cabins.

Then he saw her.

On platform four he saw a woman sitting on a bench. She was soaked through and had a case next to her feet. She looked rather sad and wasn't wearing her wig. He stood up straight to get a better look at her; it was her.

"Nelly!" he shouted. He didn't dare move or even twitch just in case he lost sight of her. She had turned to look around. He saw her saddened expression turn to hopefulness and as the final cabin went passed between them she caught sight of him. She had been crying; not that anyone would have noticed with her sopping wet hair and clothes. Richard could tell though. He always could tell.

She walked towards the edge of platform four but faltered at the line that was drawn to stay back. She looked down at it as if it was a hindrance. He had found her.

II

Nelly's Morning After

Nelly woke up and found Richard lying peacefully next to her. He was lightly snoring with his arm neatly around her. She looked at her clock and realised it was almost time to leave for work. With a grown she slipped out of the bed and got dressed. It took her a moment to gather her clothes from the night before. She was still wearing his necklace. She didn't want to wake Richard so left him a note.

He didn't budge. She kissed him lightly on the forehead not wanting to leave him.

She arrived to work just two minutes before her shift and began to work like nothing had happened. She continued to check the clock and as the minutes turned to hours, she became more and more agitated until finally, something snapped. She grabbed her purse and marched to her supervisor handing in her notice.

As she walked past the women in reception, they called after her but she just gave them a wave and called back to them, "I've just got to get away." She went straight back to her flat and began to pack her things in a case. She threw her wig away and realised she didn't own a lot of items as it all fitted in her one case. She pulled out a bag wrapped in newspaper from her mattress and unravelled it, revealing the notes inside. She counted to one hundred pound and kept it aside from the rest.

Taking one last look at the apartment she had created her life in, she locked it up and knocked on the ground floor flat in which a man opened with a vest and a pair of shorts on. She tried to avoid looking.

"Here is my rent for this month with a bit extra for the inconvenience," she explained. "I'm leaving you see."

"Where ya going?"

She turned back to him, half way out of the front door. "I just have to get away." She paused. "I'm not very good with goodbyes."

She walked briskly out the door and headed to the other side of town. As she was leaving she heard her landlord ask what happened to her hair. That made her smile. As she continued to pace through the streets, it looked like there was going to be a down pour.

She arrived at the hotel Richard had been staying in and went straight to the desk. The receptionist explained that he had already left about ten minutes ago. Nelly checked the clock and it was twenty minutes until his train.

By the time she reached the station, the down pour had begun and in her hurry, she did not try and take cover. After paying for the ticket, the ticket collector explained she needed to be on platform four so she ran along platform three and clamoured over the metal bridge, slipping by the amount of puddles that had formed everywhere around her. She leapt off the final step from the bridge and ran for the train as fast as she could, but the train was already chuffing away.

She had missed it. Watching her train disappear around a bend, she slumped onto a bench with a tear falling from her face. It was masked by the rain. Her heart sank. She allowed the rain to wash away her tears.

Nelly had not realised she had been sitting there for so long, but she heard a distant voice call her name. She looked around for a moment and stood up.

She thought she might have imagined it because there was so much noise by the train on platform three or if could have been one of her *visitors*. But then she saw him staring. She felt his eyes following her every move. It was Richard.

III

Together, they are Most Powerful

Richard gestured to her that he was going to climb the metal steps to cross over to platform four. As he did so he tripped over his case he had put down. He knocked his head with his hand to highlight his clumsiness and saw Nelly laugh at him. With his case, he ran up the steps –

two at a time and met Nelly in the middle as he saw her appearing up the other set of stairs from platform four.

Both dropped their cases and clung to each other tightly. Richard lifted her in his arms and muttered something she couldn't quite comprehend.

"You're soaked through!" he commented when he put her down. "Here take my coat." He began to take his coat off.

"No! No, don't be silly." Nelly replied placing her hands on his shoulders and straightening his coat.

"Well, you can take my hat then." He plonked it onto her head. "I thought I had lost you again."

"Me too. I missed your train by a moment!" her eyes twinkled with her rain soaked face, although still blotchy from the tears. Richard's hat slipped over the eyes and they both pushed it back in place on her head, making them giggle. "I'm glad I did now though."

Richard smoothed his hand over her cheek and spoke softly. "I've been offered a position in Cardiff and I was going to consider it. It's close to Mum and I know she would be happy to have you around again."

"What was stopping you?"

"Well, if I were to take the job, I get given a house – a family house; too big for one person."

“So what were you thinking?” Nelly moved closer to too him and he wrapped his arms round her.

“Well, Nelly, my Nelly, would you do the honour of being my wife Nell?”

“Richard, you have been so kind to me all these years.” She began. “I don’t want you to regret asking-”

“Never!” he interrupted. “Nell, I love you; you know that.”

“But what about my um, condition?”

“I love you even more because of it.” He went down on knee.

“Don’t,” Nelly whispered going red in the face. She rubbed her left arm, feeling the cloth under her clothes. Richard opened his case, pulling out some scissors and he spoke again.

“You my darling are the love of my life! Will you marry me?”

And with tears in her eyes she replied, “I will.” In that moment he cut the cloth from her arm.

Chapter Twenty Five: 2014 – An Old Man's End

"We were married next May," Richard commented, still sitting in his arm chair by the window. "I took that job in Cardiff and we lived next door to my Mum. We spent most evenings round hers though." He smiled at the memory.

Richard had completed his story of his first patient. Kirsty had just popped to the loo for a moment, but when she returned, she saw a woman standing in front of him, offering her hand to take his. "Richard?" Kirsty said with the sound of concern.

The woman smiled. She was quite elderly, with her hair was almost white and her clothes were out of place. "I told you my wife would come for me," Richard did not turn as he spoke but continued to gaze at the woman in front of him.

"Richard, your wife died remember?" Kirsty tried to reassure him.

"I told you I would be back for you," the woman said. Kirsty moved closer.

Richard's old creaky bones clicked as he stood up. He was wearing an old fashioned blue suit. His hat had been resting on his lap during today's part of the story. Richard took his wife's hand and he stood up a young man, leaving the old man in the arm chair. The old lady had also morphed into a young woman. Kirsty saw the frail old man's hand drop as the young man appeared from him. With her mouth open in shock, she saw the young man kiss his wife and hold her in his arms once again.

"Thank you Kirsty," he said turning to her. "For listening to my story."

"So this is your first patient?" she breathed aghast.

"I haven't been called that for so long, it feels odd," Nelly smiled. She lifted her sleeve and showed the scarring on her arm from where the armband used to be. "Sometimes I still think it's there and have to check."

"So the story; it is true."

"Of course," Richard spoke with a distance, although both he and Nelly had not moved. "But I was just a patient of hers as she was of mine. I needed to tell someone the story before I could see her again and I thank you for that."

"I can't believe what I'm seeing!" Kirsty sat down.

"I've been waiting by his side for so long," Nelly said. Kirsty glimpsed the discolouring of her eyes – one green and one blue. "Waiting for his mind to open to the possibility of seeing beyond the physical and you helped him."

"Now we need to take a detour before we go," Richard said taking his wife's hand.

“Where?” Nelly turned to him and her sixties dress ruffled.

“Just a quick visit to a little frightened girl. A girl who became very special to me.” He smiled with a knowing grin and Nelly kissed him on the cheek.

Nelly had understood, finally, after all these years, who the old man was when she first arrived in the asylum. Richard had been with her all her life. Even when she did not realise it was him.

Kirsty also realised Richard was going to visit Patient 2.5.7. And then the penny dropped. She knew the point of the story. It wasn’t about madness or death. It was about helping the deceased show they loved the people they left behind and finished what they started. It was about being there for someone.

“You were here the whole time,” Kirsty said. She heard Nelly’s voice within her mind as she watched them disappear.

“The loneliest of people may not be alone at all. I never was. Alone in a room; alone with your thoughts; alone in your bed. Just in the corner of your eye or a noise you thought was just your imagination. There is always someone there. Waiting. Wanting. Scared. Angry. Even lonely. You don’t admit to seeing flashes of something you do not understand, whether it be your past or your future. Accept it or deny it; it does not matter; because whatever you felt or saw at that moment, it was there and always will be within your memory and you'll think about it from time to time. It may even frighten you, but don't let it stop you. It never stopped me."

The couple smiled again at one another and hand in hand, they walked into a misty light, where they disappeared into nothing. Kirsty went to the old man in the chair; there was no pulse; he was gone. He had something in his hand however. Kirsty picked it up. It was an old, frayed piece of cloth that had been stained and weathered over the years. It read Nelly; it wasn't the numbers. There was no longer a patient called 2.5.7. Was there ever?

45081383R00151

Made in the USA
Charleston, SC
12 August 2015